The Death of Santa Claus
&
Other Stories

Books by Carol Adler

Non-Fiction

Writers, Authors & Dreamweavers: I Heard Your Call For Help – How To Write Non-Fiction, Fiction, Poetry, Memoirs, Children's Stories... And More

Do You Really Need To Write A Book?

How To Publish & Market A Book Without Jumping Off A Cliff

Fiction

The Woman With Qualities
Come As You Are
Slouching Past Bethlehem
The Extinctive Life

Poetry

Arioso: Selected Poems By Carol Adler
Shaelot: Questions
Naked In Daylight
Jesus & The Tooth Fairy/Free Radicals

The Death of Santa Claus
&
Other Stories

Carol Adler

Dandelion Books, LLC
www.dandelion-books.com

A Dandelion Books Publication

The Death of Santa Claus & Other Stories, by Carol Adler
ISBN 978-1-934280-99-7
LC Number 2012939605
Hard Copy Version

Dandelion Books, LLC
www.dandelion-books.com

To all my friends, relatives & others who have peopled my imagination throughout my 73 years. Without you, these stories never would have been written. You are amazing!

PREFACE

Even though more than half of these stories were published in literary and general readership magazines—this was before the Internet—since then I have revised most of them. I find it amazing how much I thought I knew about writing and how much I've continued to learn during the past forty years of ghostwriting, book doctoring and editing fiction and non-fiction works for others. My clients have been my best teachers!

"The Death of Santa Claus" and "Covenant" are true stories. They really happened. Both "Exegesis" and "The Puzzle" are basically true but the storyteller in me felt compelled to embellish each of them.

"Minhag," written in Sholem Aleichem folktale style, is a true story that was told to me by my ex-husband. His father was the Ober Kantor of the Mannheim, Germany Synagogue before the Holocaust brought the family to the United States. As I stated at the conclusion of that story, I never met his father, Cantor Hugo Chaim Adler.

The seed for "Yom Kippur" was planted during my early years of marriage when I was a member of my ex-husband's choir at Temple Emanu-El in Dallas, Texas. As a young bride, these wonderful people became my second family and I became very close with many of them. In the story, "Bertha" is one of the women who sat in the alto section with me. She was married to a brilliant scientist who also sang in the choir. I adored both of them. At age 40, this woman became ill with a rare blood disease and died shortly after.

The rest of the stories are pure fiction but each is laced with my personal experiences as a writer. In "Ingenue" and "Therefore I Am," the protagonist is, in fact, a writer.

—Carol Adler, Mesa Arizona

CONTENTS

THE DEATH OF SANTA CLAUS

The classroom was silent except for the tap-tapping of the chalk moving across the board as Dr. Peters, a thin balding red-haired philosophy instructor with wire-frame glasses proceeded to cover all three slates with complex configurations.

When he was finished, he swiveled around and faced the class. "Starting over at the left panel: X equals S.C. The proposition X equals the proposition Santa Claus does not exist. X equals Y. Santa Claus is the proposition X equals Santa Claus does not exist."

I flipped to a blank page in my notebook and started copying.

"Before us we see an extraordinary cosmological phenomenon." Dr. Peters cleared his throat. "A universe consisting of three kinds of facts: Phi-a or RB or S (A, b, o). Let only objects of immediate acquaintance be particulars. The statement mirrors the sense data. There are, however, many cases in which the sentence does not mirror the fact. Consider the sentence, 'Santa Claus does not exist.'"

Dr. Peters paused and glanced around the room to see how many students were impressed with what he had just uttered and how many had fallen asleep.

"This is not a mirror picture of a fact. Santa Claus is not a logically proper name," he plowed bravely on. "If it were, then Santa Claus would exist and the statement would be false. Santa Claus equals the x such that phi-x does not exist, and it's not the case that (x) (y) (phi=y=x)."

Amazing, I thought, obediently copying all three slates. All one had to do is write down a few letters and numbers, build in some weird looking symbols linked to a series of formulas and any-thing in the universe could instantly be created—or wiped out. If I took an eraser right now to all of Dr. Peters's chicken scratching, in less than five minutes it would be gone—and so would all of Dr. Peters's hard work… maybe even Dr. Peters himself.

What this brilliant young unintelligible instructor did not know and had no reason to know, I mused later as I trudged across the Quad toward the University of Michigan undergraduate library, was that in my earlier days when the world was still a giant 'X' and when both "hypothesis" and "necessary conclusion" were still hiding in the ethers of my subconscious, I had actually witnessed first-hand, "the fact that" Santa Claus really *did* exist. Not only did he exist; he would never die.

Large wet snowflakes eddied and swirled around me, collecting on my mittens and books. A bicycle bell clanged from behind and I moved to one side, letting it skid past. Amazing skill that guy had, besides being downright nervy to ride a bike on a night like this.

But why not? Who says it's snowing? Me? God? Who says the sidewalks are slick with ice? All one needs is just a few x's and y's to create a hypothesis that can easily be proved—or disproved. Like The Death of Santa Claus.

A blast of wind shot through my storm coat, pushing me forward. This cold was definitely real, I decided.

I stomped on the rubber mat outside the library to shake off the snow from my boots before pushing through the heavy glass doors to the warm brightly lit interior.

It was the week before exams so already at 7PM almost every seat was taken. The older library next door would probably be empty and was definitely a better choice tonight if I wanted to plow through that philosophy assignment and finish it. It was such a barn, so cold and drafty... but I had another reason for avoiding that library.

_____

It was December, 1942 and I was four years old. We were on our way to Noah's Ark, my older sister Tammi had informed me before we'd piled into the car. "Because Noah's Ark has the best discounts," she added wisely. "And also because the owner is Jewish," she finished. "Mrs. Noah is Mama's second cousin."

Tammi, who was a year older, knew so much more than I did. "They have rubber tires," she declared, "and ball bearing roller skates! It's s'posed to be a s'prise," she finished in a whisper as Mama bustled into the room with our snowsuits.

"But remember, Mama said not from Santa Claus this year," she whispered hastily as we bundled into the car.

Not from Santa Claus, I repeated to myself, remembering last night's conversation at the supper table. Mama hadn't told us why he wasn't coming this year, just that he wasn't. Yet when she told us about it, she didn't seem sad. He was "just disappearing," she'd said.

We were caught in heavy traffic in the middle of a snow storm. When we'd started out the streets were clean and the sky was clear, but soon after we turned onto the main thoroughfare, dark clouds appeared. A sudden frenzy of thick wet flakes was already layering car tops and blanketing the street. We inched forward behind the long line of slowly moving vehicles.

I burrowed into my snowsuit, happy to be warm and safe inside the car. I loved listening to the muted sound of the tire chains clank-clanking through the snow and watching the snowflakes chase each other past the car windows. They seemed to have a life of their own, dancing through the air, whisking and frisking round and around before melting or getting lost in the blurred clusters of yellow car lights.

Tammi and I were in the back seat squeezed between Aunt Jennie on one side and Grandpa on the other.

Aunt Jennie was one of my mother's older sisters. A tiny woman with frizzy salt-and-pepper hair, she wore lots of lipstick and could talk and smoke cigarettes at the same time. In the winter Aunt Jennie draped a six-headed raccoon fur piece around her neck. The raccoon heads hung down over her coat. Cautiously I made direct eye contact with the two beady black eyes closest to me. I'd learned already that of the six heads only four of them bit.

Slipping off my mitten, I crawled my finger up, up, up to the pointed nose—*snap!*

Aunt Jennie let out a giggle. "You thought that one was dead, didn't you, honey? Ha! Ha! Fooled you!" Scooping up one of the heads, she grabbed my bare hand and pushed it close to the animal's mouth. "Here! Put your finger here!"

"NO!" I yelped, jerking away.

"It doesn't hurt," she snorted. "Do you want me to show you where I push the button that makes them bite?"

"No," I said tearfully.

"Let me do it!" Pushing in front of Grandpa, who sat on the other side of Aunt Sophie, boldly Tammi placed a small pink finger between the open jaws of the animal. "Hey, *ouch!*" she yelped.

"Gotcha!" my aunt shouted gleefully, pretending to carefully examine Tammi's finger as my sister continued to howl.

"Okay, that's enough, both of you." Aunt Jennie pushed us away, wrapping the fur piece tightly around her neck and scrounging in her purse for her cigarettes and lighter.

In the dark my grandfather gazed munificently ahead and down the street at nothing in particular. My four years of wisdom had already informed me that Grandpa lived somewhere else. His conversation consisted of comments about the weather and the statement, "Be careful!" issued whenever he thought it necessary that we hear it.

I was already looking forward to this Saturday when a freshly cut tree, its limbs still oozing sap, would be clamped onto the trunk of the car and driven home, dragged through the back door and hammered into the wooden stand.

Tinsel-draped and glowing with multi-colored lights, the pungent odor of the dying tree would fill the house for the next few weeks.

"From now on the tree will be it," my mother had proclaimed two days ago at the dinner table.

"What do you mean, 'the tree will be it'?" I asked.

"No gifts. Just the tree. Come on, you two. Finish up. Eat the rest of your peas, Tammi."

"No gifts?" I repeated.

"What I mean is, yes, there will be gifts," said my mother, "but not on Christmas. The gifts will happen on Hanukah this year, instead of Christmas."

My Christian father looked up from his preoccupation with polishing off a second helping of mashed potatoes and blinked. From the expression on his face, apparently this pronouncement was a piece of news to him as well.

"It is time for Santa Claus to disappear," my mother finished, a note of authority in her voice that was a warning to anyone who wanted to contradict her.

Carefully I took in each word, not understanding and not wanting to. What really mattered, I told myself, were the gifts. And the tree. It would be Christmas with a tree, Mama said, but without Santa. This year, though, they would be Jewish instead of Christian gifts. I'd learned to read and write when I was three, so I already knew that "Hanukah" was Jewish for Christmas and Christmas was also spelled "Xmas" like "Xans" for "Christians." Hanukah also had two spellings. You could put a "C" in front of the "H" and it became "Chanukah."

Actually, I couldn't find anything really terrible about the change from one name to another, especially since Hanukah came before Christmas this year by *a whole week*, and Hanukah was celebrated for eight days. Eight days of gifts instead of only one!

The best part of all was that we now had two Xmases, a Jewish one and a Xan one.

I'd already learned that anything that was Jewish not only had something to do with Mama and her family, but also with the War and a terrible man named Hitler.

Except for Mama's parents, my grandmother and grandfather who lived with us [Daddy's parents lived in their own house], I thought her family was very strange. But then, so were my Xan aunts and uncles and cousins. So maybe I was strange too, I decided. Maybe everyone is... and maybe I was the strangest of all because I was *both* Jewish and Xan.

Hitler was a German and he killed Jews. He burned them in furnaces and ovens. I'd overheard Grandma talking about it one day at her bridge club. The bridge club met once a week at our house and Grandma let me pass the mints and caramels.

On the way to Noah's Ark, carefully I processed all my new information. This year the gifts would be delivered by someone who was not Santa, and they would be delivered on Hanukah, which was going to happen one week before *December 25.*

One thing I still wasn't sure about. What had happened to Santa? Why wasn't he coming? Was Santa Jewish too? Had he gone to Germany to deliver presents and maybe gotten killed there, by Hitler and the War?

At the bridge club, Grandma had said that Hitler and the War might be coming to the United States, but "we're not going to let that happen," she added quickly, giving my head a quick pat when she realized I was standing at her elbow with the mint dish.

"There!" Tammi interrupted my thoughts, pointing triumphantly out the window at the large red brick building on the left side of the street.

Racing across the panel of windows at the top of the building were huge orange and scarlet flames. Hundreds, maybe thousands of tongues lashed against the glass, devouring themselves over and over, each time shooting higher and still higher until I thought they must be racing through every part of the inside of that building.

I could almost feel the heat and hear the hissing and scraping, crackling of burning wood, crash of the walls caving in... and wailing of sirens like the Air Raid Drill sirens that were happening more often than they used to.

The traffic light turned red and the car came to a stop directly next to the burning building. Terrified, I stared at the band of visible flames, unable to look away because I knew somewhere deep down, that *I was supposed to witness this devastating scene.*

Where were the fire trucks? Surely they should have been here by now! Was there no one to fight the blaze? No one to rescue the burning bodies?

Then, suddenly the truth settled over me, penetrating my entire four-year-old being with a terrible understanding.

This burning was the reason why the streets, buildings, schools and churches were decked with X-mas wreaths and X-mas holly, X-mas candles, bells, candy, stockings and canes. It was the reason why Santa Claus wasn't coming this year and why he had disappeared.

Santa was inside that building with his wife, Mrs. Claus, and they were burning to death.

Of course no one would rescue them! *They were supposed to die, because they were Jewish.*

Too late, too late, wailed the sirens, screaming past. Even They wouldn't stop. Of course not.

My mind raced through every piece of knowledge I had ever learned about Santa. Aunt Jennie had once said that he was also called "St. Nick" and St. Nick was the devil. "You're either a devil or a saint," she told us.

I didn't know anything about saints except that Daddy, who was one hundred percent Xan, didn't believe in them. At least he said he didn't. But he didn't believe in the devil either, he said.

So maybe Santa was neither. Yet why was he burning to death? Just because he was a Jew? And Mrs. Claus too?

"It's what Xans do," Tammi had told me importantly when I'd asked her about Hitler's ovens. "They burn Jews in order to make candles they can light in front of their saints. Did you ever smell the inside of a church? I have," she boasted. "It smells like Daddy's dirty socks and Grandma's limburger cheese."

But Aunt Jennie wouldn't have called St. Nick a devil if he was a Jew, I concluded. No, I decided firmly. This was different. And worse. It was the *Jews* who had killed Santa, because they had to. He was ruining Mama's Hanukah.

It was his robe that had caught fire. His red and white fur-trimmed robe. Then he'd fallen out of his sleigh, down to earth, right through the chimney and into the furnace of that red brick building. He was a wicked cruel man who captured Jewish children in his big black bag and carried them off to the ovens.

No! I argued, choking back my tears and shaking my head. No! Not kind, generous, jolly St. Nick, who brought presents and sweets to all who were good... not jolly twinkle-eyed Santa who only yesterday was making toys at the North Pole and wrapping colorful packages—No!

4

You didn't see that sign on his belt, did you? taunted a voice inside. *His belt has one of those black "S" things right in the middle, over his stomach.*

The flames leaped before my eyes, higher and higher in all directions, leaking through the walls of the burning building and racing into the street, gobbling up traffic, cross-traffic, consuming every vehicle that was halted in front, behind and everywhere around me in that moment of time that now stood still forever.

Bareheaded, with all the courage and bravado that a four year old could muster, I strode into the light as the truth blazed before me. Now all I could see were terrified faces, thousands of them struggling in the flames, their charred arms and legs thrust into the air every which way before they went flying off into the ethers.

Overcome by feelings of sadness and loss, I realized with the greatest conviction that the voice inside was right, after all. Apparently Santa had more than one belt with an "S" buckle and all of them had been placed in a thick black band that was now moving along the top of the blazing windows.

What about the children? Had they escaped or were they also burning alive, suffocated in Santa's great black bag?

The sirens wailed in the distance, refusing to be silenced. Soon they would be ashes, carted out from the little door beneath this huge furnace like the furnace at home. Then they would be strewn across the street, used to melt the snow and ice, to let the traffic move easier.

"Sarah's going to be sick," shrilled Aunt Jennie. "All I need is to have her throw up on my coat. Come, honey. Here, honey, sit up. Papa, give her some gum. Here's some peppermint gum. Beechies."

Aunt Jennie was a secretary. She always chewed gum when she typed so she always kept gum in her purse. Why did she have to ask Grandpa to give me some of his?

It stopped snowing as suddenly as it had begun. Traffic picked up speed and we crunched forward into the Noah's Ark parking lot where Tammi and I were instructed to wait in the car with Grandpa.

Memories were like ashes... *"strewn across the streets of the mind and used to melt the snow and ice, to let the traffic move easier..."*

"Friction must be prevented at all costs," my father had said once when he was helping me with a high school science experiment.

"Yet a wheel won't turn without it," I'd argued hotly. "Friction is necessary in order for anything to move forward!"

My father smiled proudly at me. He was happy I'd inherited his passion to dig for the truth, to ask questions and ask for proof or clarification whenever something didn't seem to ring true.

I'd never asked about him and Mama, maybe because I didn't want to know. Or maybe because I needed no explanation to realize it had been a giant piece of friction for my father to leap out of his Xan vehicle, snow chains or no, and pull my mother into the passenger seat beside him at a time when intermarriage was socially taboo.

That may have been the last piece of friction he had ever dared, I thought sadly as I pulled off my woolen scarf, spread out my storm coat on the back of one of the empty wooden chairs and dumped my book bag on the large oak reading table. I was right. The old library was practically empty.

I'd never seen any smoke pouring out of the top of that building. *But that's the way it should have been,* I reminded myself as I pulled out my philosophy notebook. *Because there can never be any evidence. Not even from a burning Santa Claus. No one is supposed to know. It was part of the mystery. Part of the X that is so completely self-contained.*

And *that* was the secret. The surprise. No one should ever know because no one really *did* know.

I opened my notebook. "Let only the object of immediate acquaintance be particulars. The X such that phi-x does not exist..."

Gazing up at the high-ceilinged reading room, my eyes rested on the black swastika and floral motif that repeated itself in a decorative band around the entire perimeter of the room.

On one of the windowpanes the frost had formed a radial spoke with a target in the middle, as if some round hard object had struck the glass and ricocheted. The wind whistled harshly around the corners of the building, pushing against the stone exterior and seeping into the dank-smelling room. The lights flickered and a muffled siren shrieked into the night.

Out of the corner of my eye I was startled to see Dr. Peters's fiery red head about to duck beneath one of the reading lamps of a table several rows ahead. Before seating himself he glanced around the room. Although our eyes met, there was no recognition.

COVENANT

"Moses was a goy." "You mean Jesus." "No. I mean Moses." "Jesus had a Jewish name."

"Says who?" Dave aimed a spitball and fired it across the room. It landed in the centerfold of the open bible on Lester's desk.

The sideshows in confirmation bible class today were more creative than usual. We were restless and bored. Tomorrow was Thanksgiving and school vacation had already started yesterday. Friday was a school dance and we still had so much planning to do...

Today we were reviewing the chapters of Genesis that dealt with Abraham and the covenant. Peppered with too many "thee's" and "thou's," it was far from easy reading and these chapters in Genesis were unfamiliar. My mother owned a moth-eaten copy of the Jewish Old Testament, but it had been shoved to the back of the bookcase. I'd found it one day by accident but had never pulled it out to read it.

The only religious education I'd had before now consisted of watered-down stories about Suffering or Wandering Jews. With crayons and paints we made stick drawings of the Hebrews plodding through the desert—40 years!—or hauling bricks as slaves in Egypt. Throughout history they seemed to be losers.

Bar and bat mitzvah had not yet been added to the Reform Jewish menu and services, held on Sunday mornings, were mainly in English. No Hebrew was taught to boys *or* girls and all the Hebrew in the services was phonetically transliterated next to each word and learned by rote.

On Chanukah we ate greasy fried potato pancakes, *latkes* that smelled up the whole house. Doctored with heaps of applesauce, they went down all right but after landing in the stomach they lay there like a bad nightmare. Then at a holiday called Purim, the Jews made prune and poppy seed filled pastries shaped like three-cornered hats. The hat pastries were called Hamentaschen ["Haman's Hats"]. Haman was a Persian tyrant who had persecuted the Jews. Someone must have thought it would be a perfect time to dress up and parade around the sanctuary taking potshots at a villain who at that time—it was 1943—was equated with Hitler ['H' for "Haman" and "Hitler"].

None of this held much excitement for me. The pastries, like the latkes were hard on the digestive track and I hated prunes. All of it seemed like so much militaristic macho at a time when boxcars of German Jews were being transported to gas chambers and made into soap. For all we knew, we might be next. By third grade I'd had my fill of Holocaust movies that the whole religious school was forced to view every week. These, along with most Jewish cooking, left a bad taste in my mouth.

At age 15, it still didn't seem like much fun being a Jew, so there I was, cutting up with my classmates and not really caring much about the bible stuff that Rabbi Rosenbusch was dutifully trying to ram down our throats before next June's confirmation. Eagerly we counted the days when all this Jewish suffering would be over, once and for all.

Added to this was the fact that I was only half-Jewish. My father was Christian and had no intention of converting. Since he had no use for any form of religion, he had no problems with my Jewish mother's decision to give my sister and me a Jewish education.

On that particular day in confirmation class we were discussing Abraham receiving the Covenant from God.

Like most of my classmates, I'd been through the usual pubescent capers, but at that age it was more or less the blind leading the blind. Except for art museum visits and photographs of Grecian sculptures, anatomy drawings, etc.—without any brothers or close male cousins and surely no traumatic experiences of incest or rape—I had no frame of reference when it came to viewing a full-grown male with his pants off. It just hadn't happened.

I raised my hand.

"Sarah?"

"Rabbi, in Genesis 17:1," I began, "there's one word I don't understand concerning the covenant God made with Abraham. God says, 'This is My covenant, which ye shall keep, between Me and you and thy seed after thee: every male among you shall be circumcised.' I'd like to know what He means, or what the word 'circumcised' means."

A toxic silence fell over the room. All whispering and chattering stopped and Rabbi Rosenbusch grew visibly pink. Several class members openly giggled.

I was puzzled. This was certainly not intended to be funny. I was asking a legitimate question. Until I'd read this bible passage, I'd never seen the word "circumcised" before. Certainly the word never would have been used in my Jewish-Christian non-religious home and unfortunately, before coming to class, I hadn't taken time to look it up in a dictionary. I suppose that was because I thought it was an archaic word that no one else would have been familiar with either, and that would easily be defined by the rabbi. Why bother doing the research myself?

Yet here we were, almost all the way through today's session and Rabbi Rosenbusch had never even referred to the word. In fact, when he mentioned "The Covenant" it was as if he took it for granted that we all knew what it meant.

"Yes. Well." Rabbi Rosenbusch cleared his throat. "It is the—er, ritual—er—operation that occurred that time for the uh first time in history whereby the uh male foreskin was er-uh, *removed* from the male organ. It is as you know a—uh—special ceremony called a 'bris' that is performed today on every Jewish male infant eight days after they are born. 'Bris' as you know is—uh—the Hebrew word for 'covenant.' Shall we move on? Next chapter, please."

Was it the silence or the slamming of my blood? Did the hands of the large clock on the wall stop moving? The room started spinning as a series of vignettes flashed before my eyes.

It was Chanukah and/or Christmas. My sister and I were standing next to our enormous, thickly icicled tree in front of a tin menorah. Lined up under the tree were nine red and green, blue and yellow wrapped packages. Excitedly we ripped off the wrapping. In each of the packages was a large pink wax replica of a penis.

"What are they?" my sister asked me, because of course I would know what they were, wouldn't I? I was very smart, and anyway, the rabbi had just told me. I also knew what was to be done with them.

Lifting the wax penises from their boxes, carefully I inserted each of them in one of the empty holes of the menorah. The ninth hole was higher than the others, so the penis I would place there would be called the *shamos,* or leader because it would light the wicks of the lower ones. This wax penis was different from the rest. It was large and floppy-looking at the tip, as if the candle maker had forgotten to trim it. In order for it to hold a flame, I would have to carve away some wax from the wick.

Taking a knife, I gouged a hole in the center and lopped off a large chunk of pink wax.

Next, I saw my 15 year old blonde, Gentile-and-Jewish body in an Aphrodite pose in front of the mirror stark naked, but with a strange aberration.

Emerging from the clump of hair between my legs was a prominent male-looking organ. It was so long it almost touched the ground.

Tied around it was a large pink bow.

My mother emerged from the shadows and stood directly in front of me. Peering over her shoulder was my father, who was timidly eying the oversize organ and me. Then, both my father and I turned at the same time to stare with horror at the long sharp knife my mother was brandishing in front of me. It was the meat knife that my father sharpened every week in order to carve whatever version of roast was placed in front of him on the Sunday table.

I was amazed that when the knife made contact with the penis and my mother neatly sliced it off at the base, I felt no pain.

Carefully she wiped off both the penis and the knife on her red-checkered apron and handed both items to my father.

In the third scene my father was naked and he was arguing with my mother. He was apparently furious because his neck and ears were flaming red. Whenever he got angry only his neck and ears—never his face—got red. His mouth was twitching uncontrollably as he shouted and gesticulated in a manner highly uncharacteristic of him. I do not recall my father ever waving his arms, or for that matter, shouting at my mother.

My mother didn't seem to be listening because she was shrieking at the top of her lungs and repeating over and over what I made out as a single word: **"Bris."**

Since this word as well as the word "circumcised" had just been explained to me by the rabbi, I now knew what my mother was talking about. She was referring to that Special Ceremony, the Very Same Ceremony that God had performed on Abraham in order to initiate him as the leader and patriarch of His Chosen People—thereafter known as The Israelites.

My mother was apparently determined to play God. Kneeling in front of my father and pushing aside his hands so she could grab a firm hold of his penis, slowly and deliberately she started to work. Carefully she moved her knife around the tip as if she were peeling a carrot, slowly cutting away the skin. Then at a certain point, deftly she ripped off the flap from the rest of my father's organ.

I was surprised that nothing gushed out when my mother inserted the knife and proceeded to rip and cut. I was also surprised that my father didn't simply keel over from shock and pain.

On the contrary. As she continued to work on him, his rage seemed to vanish. Within seconds he grew amazingly calm. His arms dropped passively to his sides and his mouth straightened. Dreamily he closed his eyes. I watched the angry flush drain from his ears and neck. A tiny Mona Lisa smile of pleasure appeared on his face. He was enjoying it!

When my mother had finished, she held up the severed piece of skin for my father to see. Then, as I had never seen him do before—he was not a demonstrative man—he scooped her up in his arms and smothered her with passionate kisses.

My next vignette featured the rabbi, now dressed in white. Apparently he was no longer a rabbi but a surgeon. A large round disc had been strapped to his head and he was peering at me through the disc.

I was naked, stretched out on my back on a long white paper covered table. To my horror, as the surgeon continued to hover over me, I discovered that a growth resembling a male organ was starting to emerge from the surgeon's disc. The protrusion grew longer... and longer... it was now very large and round and hard.

The surgeon straightened, the organ bobbing up and down, and shook his head regrettably. The organ also bobbed up and down and shook regrettably. He turned to my mother, who was standing to one side of the table apparently waiting eagerly for a verdict.

"I'm sorry," he sighed, "but it's just not there. She is undeniably a girl, and girls don't have them. To my knowledge, there is as yet no way of correcting God's work, unless of course, you pray. And since I'm not a rabbi, I'm hardly equipped. You could also pretend. I've known several patients who have been quite successful, using a number of methods: EST, Gestalt, TM, Biofeedback... or you could always have her strap one on..."

The final vignette was of several multicolored penises, dozens of them in varying sizes and shapes representing the whole gamut of human possibilities from every culture, every race and ethnicity, dancing in a ring.

They were linked or stitched together by the tiny flaps of skin that had only partially been removed from the tips of their organs.

To my surprise I was in the center of the circle and I was being celebrated. As the penises danced, they shouted out in familiar gutturals the watchword of the Jewish People—My People: *Shema Yisrael, Adonai Eloheinu, Adonai Echad...*

This is the one command or exhortation that throughout the ages had served to either execute or redeem the Jews in the name of Their God—and in the name of Our Male Ancestors: Abraham, Isaac and Jacob.

At last the bell rang.

In the coat room Sharon, Sheldon, Eric, Jim, Janice, Dave and JoAnne—the whole class crowded close, pounding me on the back and congratulating me.

"Sarah, that was brilliant! Really brilliant," giggled Eleanor, whose 100% Jewish family owned one of the largest and most exclusive department stores in the city. Rarely did Eleanor speak to me unless she had to.

I knew the silent question all my classmates were asking was: *How did I, usually the Goody Two Shoes of the class, ever get up enough nerve to make such a fool of Rabbi Rosenbusch?*

"Did you see how shook up he was? I mean, like, man he really didn't know *what* to say—and the best part of all," Dave crowed, "was that you didn't even crack a smile. I mean you were really deadpan! You should've *seen* the expression on your face! He really thought, I mean he *believed,* you were serious!"

"Hey Sarah, what did you get on the Math quiz? You're such a brain, you probably broke the curve and got a hundred. You want a ride home instead of taking the bus? My dad's picking me up; he won't mind dropping you off."

"Listen, Sarah, I still think if we want to get those decorations up in time we'd better get there early Friday morning. I have to be home by early afternoon to wash my hair and my mom's not through yet with my dress. I may need another fitting. So why don't we meet at the school at 9 and bring a sandwich for lunch? Then we can..."

EXEGESIS

So my father was Jesus Christ again, since Uncle Lew and Aunt Sophie had just arrived from Pittsburgh on their annual Pilgrimage to New York City with free hotel stopover at our house in Rochester. Located in "upstate New York," Rochester was considered the boonies compared to The Big Apple.

By now I'd learned that the large loaf of Jewish Rye that traveled with them was Bread with an Attitude. In addition to being crusty and somewhat sour, it was loaded with a kind of seed that was known to produce noxious gas fumes shortly after ingestion. More despicable even than the atmosphere it produced was the fact that it was totally incompatible with our Sunbeam toaster.

Even though the toaster was considered family property, it belonged mainly to my Christian father, since he was the only one who used it. My mother skipped breakfast and in the morning my sister, Tammi and I did the cheerios thing.

For as long as I can remember, this shiny pop-up plug-in kitchen device was set for producing two slices of lightly tanned White & Wonderful toast promptly at 7:41AM, which, after being buttered, was cut into eight neat squares and placed on a green Aztecware plate where it served as the foundation for two perfectly poached smiley faced eggs.

As soon as Uncle Lew had dumped the bagels, lox, gfilte fish, knishes and rye bread on the kitchen counter, while my father was outside hauling in their luggage and schlepping it into the sunroom where they would sleep on the rollout bed, he picked up the toaster and slid the lever to HI, which stood for Dark.

The next morning, since my father was always the first one up and it was Saturday—no one except my father ever had breakfast on Saturday before mid-morning—at 7:30AM he entered the kitchen and went about his usual morning ritual. Soon the coffee pot was perking away, the water was boiling in the poached egg cooker, the stainless steel poachers had been buttered and prepared for the eggs, the green Aztecware plate was ready to receive the toast—everything was moving along smoothly.

Note that for my father's White & Wonderful breakfast, timing is everything. The eggs are poaching as the bread is being toasted. The eggs are ready as soon as White & Wonderful pops up out of the toaster. I don't recall ever knowing anyone who enjoyed cold poached eggs.

Before I continue, let me make one point clear. My father is not anti-Semitic. He has the greatest respect for Jews and Judaism. He was never a practicing Christian, if that would matter, so he would not have even thought about objecting when my mother told him that her [their] children would be raised Jewish.

Like many Christians, my father has no objection to co-existing with any other person in the universe, regardless of their race, religion or background, as long as they have manners. On the other hand, he openly detests anyone who happens to be Chutzpadik, a Yiddish term for pushy, rude, arrogant, ill-mannered, self-centered, inconsiderate and unkind, and who thinks they can barge into any person's home or private life and take over their toaster.

Anyone can be Chutzpadik; they don't have to be Jewish. Often these individuals are displaced persons from a rapid transplant. Left without any frame of reference, they cling to whatever gastronomic refugees they can conjure up from the past. Pasta for the Italians, sausage for the Poles, and smoked whitefish and rye bread for the Jews.

These native foods are their security blankets, and like their god(s), are superior to all other people's security blankets and gods. As a fourth generation Wasp, my father's security blankets were loaves of White & Wonderful for peanut butter and tuna fish salad sandwiches, and two slices *lightly toasted* for the 7:45AM Poached Egg Program.

Predictably, the Chutzpadik believes their food, restaurants, hotels, lifestyle & religious rituals are better than any other. They also feel the world owes them something for having introduced their Superior God and Five-Star Security Blankets. Ironically, they are also well aware that they have nothing to offer in return but their own fear and insecurity. Maybe for that reason they always seem to function at their highest level when they are seeking "something for nothing." For example, my aunt and uncle, who made a good living, thought nothing of descending upon our modest one-bathroom house whenever they pleased. Paying for a hotel room was out of the question.

On that particular morning, the toaster seemed to be taking longer than usual to produce its two perfectly tanned slices. Mildly surprised, my father waited patiently, removing the poached eggs from the stove, waiting… and waiting… 7:42… 7:43… Finally up popped two hardly White & Wonderful slices of burnt offering.

At noon when the family collected in the kitchen and Uncle Lew and Aunt Sophie were putting in their order to my father for brunch [my mother never even lifted a potholder before dinner] he turned on them, white with a fury that matched his White & Wonderful You Know What.

"Who broke the toaster? The toaster is broken!" he shouted, yanking the toaster cord from the wall. Cradling the [broken] Sunbeam in his arms, he leaped through the dining room to the living room, flung open the front door, galloped across the front lawn, and heaved it into the street.

Our house was situated on a busy thoroughfare that served as the New York State Thruway before it had been built. I was already thinking that it would have been relatively impossible even on a Saturday when traffic was lighter, to retrieve an electric toaster before it got mutilated by a string of speeding cars and trucks.

"Whoever goes after it," suggested Uncle Lew, cracking open the stunned silence, "will get a large dish of ice cream topped by The Works."

If my father is Jesus Christ, I am Mary Magdalene. I love my father dearly and deep down in every part of my being, I feel sorry for him. I feel sad that he got stuck with such terrible Chutzpadik relatives without even knowing what he was getting into.

At age nine I was hooked on sugar and especially ice cream. I happened to know that the freezer currently contained Pink Bubble Gum, Peppermint Chocolate Chip and Butterscotch Marble half gallon containers of ice cream.

"Uncle Lew, I'm your man." I stood brave and stalwart before him. "The dish will have two scoops of each of the three flavors of ice cream in the freezer. There's whipped cream and chocolate syrup in the refrigerator. You will begin creating my Reward and I expect it to be waiting for me when I return with the toaster."

I was very athletic, so the sprint across the lawn and into the street was nothing. Since I was too young to care what the neighbors thought—and besides, at that moment I was more Mary Magdalene than ever in my whole life—with lighting speed I swooped down on the toaster and retrieved it just before it was about to be smashed to smithereens by a large dump truck.

After setting it on the table next to my humongous dish of ice cream topped to my delight with not one but six maraschino cherries, in the presence of my Aunt Sophie, my mother and sister, who were acting as if they too had just been removed from the freezer—during Acts I and II of this drama

I think they had stopped breathing and were now numbly witnessing Act III—I proceeded to remove the spoon from the ice cream. Carefully and deliberately I placed it on the table.

Then, leaning forward so I was eye-to-eye with Uncle Lew, I heaved the dish of ice cream into his face.

With the rest of the family I watched it clatter to the floor. I watched the six red cherries, the frozen dollops of ice cream slide down over Uncle Lew's nose and cheeks, falling from his chin into his lap. I watched him turn Pink Bubble Gum, then Green Mint with flecks of Chocolate, and finally at the bottom of the dish, Butterscotch Marble.

Now for Act IV, the Finale and Curtain Call. I turned to my father, who was standing in the doorway—the wings—and waited for him to waltz to center stage.

With his usual neatness and propriety, he picked up the spoon from the table and placed it in the sink. Then, with all the calmness of that dude who had spent his last moments chilling out nailed to a cross, he reached for the floor mop to clean up the mess beneath my uncle's chair. After he was finished, using the same mop, he started in on Uncle Lew.

THE PUZZLE

"Where is she?"

"Yes, where is she?" smirked my older sister Tammi, mincing and swaggering up the stairs in a passable imitation of Aunt Sophie. Without knocking, she entered my bedroom and waved in front of my face the envelope she'd just snatched from Uncle Lew.

Like all of Uncle Lew's envelopes, it was long and greasy with an open slit at one end, bearing the appearance of having survived a severe paper shortage.

This one was bleeding on one side with scribbled recipes for Double-Bake Cheesecake and Never-Fail Matzoh Balls amidst a splattering of phone numbers. On the other side was a graphic display of naked breasts in assorted shapes and colors. The breasts stared fixedly back at me as I eyed the envelope with my usual suspicion.

I already knew the envelope was too flat to have anything inside except paper money or just paper. Since my uncle never gave away money, paper or otherwise, and my sister was offering it to me, I figured it must be another one of his puzzles. These were the kind of gimmicky things that demanded wits or intelligence, both of which Tammi possessed. Already at nine, however, she'd realized these tools were useless if she were to apprentice herself to Aunt Sophie.

Aunt Sophie was Uncle Lew's wife and our mother's eldest sister. I privately called her The Peacock; a name that had I been a few years older, I would have translated as "Cock Tease." At one time Aunt Sophie had been the belle of Rochester Jewish society; now at age 43, she was an arrogant bitch.

Petite and coquettish, Tammi was a cross between Debbie Reynolds and Doris Day with a pug modification of what was commonly known as a Jewish nose, enormous blue eyes and naturally blonde hair. The blonde color was her only acquisition from the ethnic ragbag that comprised our immediate family that included besides the tallit[1] and gaberdines[2] of the Litvak or Lithuanian Jew[3], our father's Anglican heritage.

I emerged from the motley DNA resembling almost to the last birth mark my Protestant father's mother who could have posed for the rosy-cheeked flaxen-haired peasant on the Dutch Cleanser[4] can.

I was not only fat and awkward; I was also inordinately smart, bordering on smart ass; with no other goals in life at age eight than to ridicule my sister's Aunt Sophie/Lana Turner/Betty Grable airs and prove one day that misanthropy would rule the world. [For the less educated, without even being prompted, I offered the following definition of a misanthrope as a person who displayed a generalized dislike, distrust, disgust, contempt or hatred of the human species.]

---

[1] *tallit* - prayer shawl

[2] Gabardines – Orthodox Jews wore black gabardine suits and black top hats. Today this is the characteristic dresss for Chasidic Jews.

[3] Lithuanian Jew –Many of the Jews from Eastern Europe came from Poland and Lithuania where they lived in ghettos; their Orthodoxy as well as their separation from non-Jews and the fact that they spoke Yiddish among themselves continued to isolate them when they emigrated to the U.S. and other countries.

[4] Dutch Cleanser – In the 1930s, this was a popular household cleansing powder.

Commonly referred to as "The Brain" and in moments of heat, "Hortense Ham Fat," I had already convinced the immediate members of the family of my precocity and was often publicly and not without pride pronounced not only brilliant but also, as with all personages who posed a threat to my parents' self-imposed insularity, supercilious and boorish.

In short, I was a bratty wunderkind quick to detect ambivalence as well as deceit; and for all that, in our matriarchal household, born into the wrong end of the spectrum where I seemed to radiate my father's latent anti-Semitism: his Calvinist aversion to alcohol and my Uncle Lew's alcoholism, and an unmitigated hatred for all members of my mother's family. Aunt Sophie and Uncle Lew ran a close first for being at the top of the list.

This was their semi-annual visit, my aunt having transported herself to another ghetto known as Squirrel Hill in Pittsburgh, Pennsylvania where bagels were purported to be fresher and bialys[5] beyond reproach. My parents, who feared any type of food adventure or for that matter, *any* adventure beyond their Saturday treks to the A & P, would never have dreamed of purchasing a few of Rochester's bagels and bialys to make the comparison.

In case anyone really wanted to know, I would self-importantly define my parents' behavior as *neophobic,* meaning "afraid of anything new."

The only thing Aunt Sophie brought with her besides her rummage sale wardrobe with its sewn-in labels from Neiman-Marcus and Bonwit-Teller, was Uncle Lew and his unquenchable thirst for good bourbon. Uncle Lew's part of the bargain would be one of these greasy envelopes and an endless run of dirty jokes. The bottle was bottomless and so was my uncle's repertoire. My father usually served as water boy, since the rest of the adults were usually either spellbound, tipsy or just plain stiff. My father was also the only one with a driver's license who was sober enough to make a run to the liquor store to replenish the supply. His treat, of course.

If asked, my father, like I, probably would have candidly admitted that we hated the jokes as well as Uncle Lew and his whiskey. Maybe that's why we were never asked.

Uncle Lew was what one would euphemously call a Retired Comedian, or someone for whom the limelight had apparently showered more than lemon and lime custard pies in The Good Old Days. In his later years we were given to witness only the gall that was slowly hardening to verdigris scabs of eventual cirrhosis. Once calcification had set in, i.e., when Borscht Belt vaudeville had been replaced by Hollywood and the Depression, he had been forced to retire into the shoe business and the newly established country club circuit. This wasn't as bad as it seemed, since it provided the right connections for my aunt, and for him, the right bourbon. Remember that internal program: "*We deserve something for nothing.*"

As soon as they arrived, the phone never stopped ringing [we were the Bed & Breakfast, Free Cash Bar w/Setups, and Social Switchboard], the liquor never stopped flowing, and my grandfather, who prided himself on his abstinence after having survived a heart attack, invariably got sick and had to be rushed to the hospital.

I often wondered when the family finally realized that Uncle Lew was not only a mediocre businessman who was scarcely scraping by, but also an alcoholic.

If it was a puzzle Uncle Lew had brought in his greasy envelope, it would be only for me because I was the perfect candidate. My father, who was a genius and could easily have solved anything Uncle Lew considered difficult, was still fixing X-Rays somewhere in the bowels of the city and wasn't due home for another hour.

---

[5] A popular type of roll characteristically associated with Jewish delicatessens, they are flavored with onion and garlic flakes, poppy seeds, sesame seeds, etc. and are used as sandwich bread for pastrami, corned beef and chopped liver.

I'd already ruled out Tammi because brain teasers or anything that was connected to the brain wasn't part of Aunt Sophie's [or her] repertoire. My mother would have also said no. In spite of her college degree and an inordinate amount of common sense, she'd long been inured to the fact that she would never be anything more than my Aunt Sophie's baby sister. Twelve years her younger and partially crippled by polio at birth, she had always been a chronic crybaby and perpetual tag-along. Now as an adult who wasn't nearly as bad looking as she believed, she still felt cheated by the god who was in charge of doling out Aunt Sophie-like high cheekbones, leggyness, cute little tits and a high and mighty behind.

It mattered little to her that it was she who had ended up with the prize: a man who was decent, kind, generous, faithful, brilliant, and long-suffering. Unlike Uncle Lew, my father didn't drink, gamble or try to be someone he was not. He was not Jewish and didn't even try to get along with Uncle Lew and his ilk. He simply ignored them. To my eight year old way of thinking, my father was qualified to run for the position of a non-Jewish Jesus Christ.

How did we ever manage during those Uncle Lew/Aunt Sophie visits with only one bathroom? Six of us with Uncle Lew's fifteen minute showers and Aunt Sophie's hour-long face creaming and hair rolling rituals, after which my father spent considerable time in the basement cleaning the trap and opening clogged pipes.

Those were not easy stays. Something invariably happened. Among the most vivid memories was an August visit when my father had returned hot and sweaty from one of his more challenging wrangles with a broken diathermy to discover my grandfather's and Uncle Lew's trout catch swimming in the bathtub. In addition to hating my Uncle Lew, my father also hated fish unless it emerged from a tin can and could be camouflaged with enough mayonnaise to create a disconnect between anything that had once been Alive and Swimming.

I'm not sure what happened to that trout; it must have made a rapid exit. I do know who ended up scrubbing the tub.

———————————

Six white paper squares, each with a large black capital letter. That's all that was inside the greasy envelope when Uncle Lew poured them from the slit. I was to tackle the puzzle while my uncle and the rest of the family hovered over me with a stop watch, breathing on the letters and me with their garlicky fire.

Six letters; six days down and two more to go before they would leave town. Six people using one small bathroom.

I was the seventh. Seven for Sheva. Sheba. Seven for seven days of the week. Sheba was Queen. The Queen of Days was Shabbat.

Was I really a genius like my father, or was this merely a local demonstration of the Law of Relativity: no one else in this family worthy of comparison?

Uncle Lew turned over all the white squares so the letters were face down. "When I say 'Go' I want you to flip over each of the letters and start putting them together to make a sentence," he instructed.

With one shove of his arm, he pushed aside my grandmother's large hand-crocheted doily. [When my English/Anglican paternal grandfather retired at age 34, my Dutch Calvinist paternal grandmother went into the doily crocheting business. Consequently, our house was a blizzard of white lace with doilies everywhere. My mother loathed the doilies almost as much as she loathed Grandma.]

My vision blurred. Was this dizziness from anticipated success, confusion—or maybe fear of failure?

I sorted out the vowels first . Three females: two 'O's and one 'A.' My mother, my sister and me. One 'D,' for "Dad," a 'J' for "Jackass" "Jerk" or "Joker"; and one 'B' for—well, okay—"Female Dog."

How long did it take? Two seconds? Three? Like some predestined oracle in which a self-appointed *spiritus mundi* had sucked me into its sphere, I breathed on the chaos and delivered the only possibility.

"'DO A JOB!'" shrieked my sister. 'DO A JOB!'"

"I told you she'd break the record, didn't I?" declared Aunt Sophie Peacock, fluttering her wings. My mother blew her nose loudly, also signaling "I told you so" to my uncle, who was already scooping up the letters and tearing the wrapper from a brand-new bottle of Johnny Walker that my father, magically appearing from the kitchen, had just placed in his hands.

Learning of my triumph but arriving too late to witness it, my father's expression was one of bewilderment and pride, as if not quite sure what to make of it and afraid to pursue it further. "Whose job?" he was probably thinking. Or, "Who's supposed to pay for it *this* time?"

"*DO A JOB*," I repeated to myself.

Of course. I should have known better. The victory, like all my victories, could only be tentative. It wasn't really mine because it wasn't Theirs. They were already onto other things that were larger and more important than solving puzzles.

My uncle and grandfather were trailing my mother into the kitchen to pick up their liquor glasses, my aunt was reaching for the telephone... when were they due for lunch at The Club?... My sister Tammi hanging on her arm and begging for just one more spray of *Muguet*....

Within seconds my father and I were the only remaining persons in the dining room. My father, now empty-handed except for the paper bag from the liquor store which he had folded into a neat rectangle; and I, empty-hearted.

Both of us hung there, not knowing whether to look at each other or at the dining room table which, now dispossessed of the puzzle and its voluminous white doily, seemed obscenely naked. I stared down at the oversize doily on the floor. In the middle of one of the hand-crocheted pineapples was the greasy blue-black heel mark of Uncle Lou's left shoe.

My father stooped down to retrieve the doily and as he straightened, our eyes met. Although he didn't drink, I saw that his eyes were webbed with little rivulets of red like Uncle Lew's, and the whites were pink and watery. From his daily exposure to X-Ray, his skin had a yellowish cast that at that moment seemed more pronounced than usual, as if pumping through his veins was not the damaged cirrhotic blood of my uncle or the royal red bloodline of my mother's Jewish ancestry, but the blood of a thoroughbred. Liquid gold, unalloyed.

"DO A JOB," said his eyes. "DO A JOB!"

MINHAG[6]

Who can deny the tenor of my voice? Pitch, range, performance, I aim for the highest. And practiced in *din*[7] I am. If Hillel could recite the whole of Torah while standing on one foot, when I am in voice I can recite any measure of notes on one foot, no feet, who cares? I'm good at what I do.

So I told myself as I traveled the road to Bad Ems to the synagogue where as a Cantor[8] I would be on *probe.*[9]

Today was Rosh Chodesh, the New Moon of Heshvan. As soon as I arrived, I would be called upon to lead the procession of the Holy Scrolls. What was this trembling inside but the morning chill?

According to my instructions, the town of Bad Ems was to my right, but as I trudged forward on the narrow road, as the night sky slowly lifted, all I could see on either side were trees and more trees. I began to wonder if I'd taken a wrong turn.

Then suddenly I came upon a certain spot where the giant firs parted and the road drew wide. Rising before me and glowing like the sun itself was the synagogue. Its great glass dome sent forth a radiance that seemed to illumine the whole of the mountainside and the town below that was slowly emerging from the mist.

And there were the people, tiny specks scarcely visible among the rising vapors, climbing up the side of the mount as they gathered for morning prayers.

———————————

Herr Himmelreich, the President of the Congregation, rushed forward to greet me, warmly clasping my hand. "Ah, Cantor! Indeed, how honored we are!" Quickly he ushered me inside; services were about to begin.

Now what awaited me in the interior of this synagogue was surely a sight which only faith could support. The Ner Tamid,[10] the candles, the lights, the very walls shimmered and glowed. And when the people rose before the Ark and the drapes drew wide and in the parting of the folds appeared the Holy Scrolls, I beheld on their faces and in their eyes that radiance that comes to dwell only among those who treasure their heritage and cherish the Law. And when the procession began and I was given one of these beloved Scrolls to cradle in my arms, I moved as if the rhythm were the step itself, myself no self but the voice that rose beyond my own in a swell of sound that freely flowed and rose so high above the rest, it was surely as high as the heavens themselves and purer than all the sounds of the earth and all that sang within.

We marched and marched, all of us, young and old—what a glorious sight! There was even a man so lame and well along in years, he could scarcely hold himself upright upon his cane; but on he

---

[6] Minhag – "tradition" in Hebrew

[7] Din – matters of litigation or law (Din Torah)

[8] Cantor - The "chanter" or vocal leader of the prayer services; also one of the wise, learned and highly revered leaders of the congregation

[9] Probe – German word meaning "Audition or trial"

[10] Ner Tamid – Eternal Light (Hebrew)

marched, his face glowing with the love and faith and inner strength that kept him marching on. We marched and sang and singing marched...

We marched until we came upon a certain place on the south side of the sanctuary six rows from the bimah.[11] And one by one, as each man approached this spot, he stopped and dipped his head, then marched on as before.

I was bewildered. Until this time I'd felt so completely at home. The ritual was my ritual, the chant my chant, the prayers my prayers... but what was this? What law was this that I didn't know about that commanded every man to dip their heads and bow when they came upon this place on the south side of the sanctuary six rows from the bimah?

As soon as the service was over, I approached the Shamos.[12] Lifting one eyebrow and folding his arms in front of him, he gazed at me for several moments without speaking. "Of course," he spoke at length, breaking the silence, "you are versed in the ritual. One takes it for granted that a Cantor... yes, er..." gesturing broadly with his hand "...surely knows the Law... One bows before the Almighty, as you know..."

"Yes, of course, my good man, of course," I said, "but why does one bow *there*, at that particular place, on the south side of the sanctuary six rows from the bimah?"

The Shamos placed a hand on my arm. "Ahh, so! Young man, I have been Shamos here for thirty years and for thirty years I have witnessed the same act. Man for man, the whole of the congregation, when they come upon that place, they bow."

Directly after morning services I set out with Herr Himmelreich, my host, in the direction of his home for noon meal. It was such a pleasant day, I was enjoying the smell of the fresh air and the pines... but at the same time I was troubled. That one ritual, that one act of bowing down on the south side of the sanctuary, six rows from the bimah... where oh where could a description of this ritual be found? Mentally I searched the Holy books of Law, the Torah, Mishneh, Gemoreh—to no avail. Nowhere could I recall any rule, any law, any dictum that stated...

"Herr Cantor," said Herr Himmelreich, breaking the silence, "if you are worried about the impression you've made, let me put your mind at rest. The people are so happy to welcome you. Your whole being speaks of love for God and Torah and mankind. You are also a very learned man, and at such a young age!"

Gratefully I pressed his hand. "You are very kind, Herr Himmelreich. Forgive me if I seem too taken with myself. And God forgive me if I appear too concerned about my impression... it is something else that is puzzling me. I am a very simple man but a pious one, praised be His Blessed Name. And you are right, I pride myself on knowledge of the Law, which is bidden me by command to obey. But tell me, Herr Himmelreich, where is it told that every man should bow before the Almighty when he stands on the south side of the sanctuary six rows from the bimah?"

"Ahh—so! Is that it?" exclaimed Herr Himmelreich, at once relieved. "Well that is a small matter, my friend. It is simply Minhag—tradition, of course!"

"Tradition," I repeated. "Tradition?"

"Ahhh, yes! On that Sacred Spot, one bows."

"Well I agree, if one bows then it is surely sacred," I said, "but why? What is the law?"

Herr Himmelreich smiled patiently, patting my arm. "Reason, Herr Cantor. Since when has reason taken precedence over faith? The spot is simply Sacred. Let us not attempt to capture the essence of what we must believe in and trust as we trust in the Law and gratefully acknowledge its Creator and Preserver, the Source of all Inspiration that is the Law Itself and is that inheritance which is ours

---

[11] Bimah (Hebrew) – alter or tower; in the synagogue it is located in the center of the synagogue; services are conducted from the bimah.

[12] Shamos (Hebrew) – leader of the congregation (administrative director)

alone, brought down to us from Mount Sinai and from the generations of those who came before us… who were and are as we are—the People of the Book. The very Bearers and Sharers…"

I glanced around behind me and up at the sky. We had changed direction in our descent, now traveling deeper into the forest. The great gold dome of the synagogue was slowly diminishing in size, then finally it disappeared altogether in the thick green bastion of firs.

"My father bowed, my father's father he bowed, and so I bow," continued Herr Himmelreich. "It is tradition to bow. My children they bow and my children's children, they too will bow. Now come and meet my wife!"

———————————————

Upon returning later to the synagogue for afternoon services, I continued to ask other members of the congregation, receiving only the same response: "It is Minhag, Tradition to bow at that spot."

Where had I fallen short of knowing the law? What piece of Holy Knowledge had somehow escaped me?

Minhag! Tradition! Was that all I was to know? Surely not enough, my heart informed me. For surely I could not serve these fine people and be one of them unless I bowed… yet I knew I could not and would not bow unless I knew the reason why.

How could I sleep a wink that night? How could I be at peace with myself ever again if I should blindly practice some sacred ritual without knowing why? Shabbos was almost here and I would be called upon to march and sing once again…

No! I declared firmly to myself. *"A man shall be commanded according to his intelligence," say the Proverbs. "He that is of a distorted understanding shall be despised… It is better to hear the rebuke of the wise, than for a man to hear the song of fools…"* Let me go before the Sofer,[13] the wisest Jew in Bad Ems, and disclose my ignorance to him.

The Sofer folded his hands over his stomach and twiddled his thumbs as he peered at me above his spectacles. "So, young man, you doubt the piety of these Jews on the basis of your own pious practices. Why is it that young men today attempt to sow their own seeds of righteousness? What is Tradition but the establishment of The Law? We are well established here in Bad Ems, and rather unwilling to change the Law, since it is, hmmm—er—God's Law and not yours. Perhaps this is not the most suitable congregation for you, after all."

"Please, my good man," I remonstrated, "you are far wiser and more learned than I could ever hope to be. It is not as it appears! I *do* wish to stay here and I have no desire to change anything—for, like you and like all pious Jews, Tradition is my bread and The Law is my meat. But I cannot be nourished by mere word of mouth, nor can it be made more palatable by any amount of reasoning or prayer unless it has some substance to begin with. Please understand, I only beg to know the reason for what is already practiced as a pious act."

"Young man," the Sofer rose and showed me to the door, "I have been Sofer here for fifteen years. For fifteen years I have dwelled here among these good people and for fifteen years I have seen no such piety as I have witnessed here in Bad Ems. When I came fifteen years ago they bowed down at that spot and for fifteen years they have continued to bow down at that same spot. It was enough for me to bow down—enough—Dayenu!"

I was stunned. The Sofer was a wise and honest man—could he not see the folly of his words? Or was I too young after all to perceive a deeper significance?

Too young! The Sofer had only been here for fifteen years. All of the learned men he had consulted had lived in Bad Ems for more than twenty-five years.

———————————————

[13] Sofer (Hebrew) – the most learned member of the congregation (scribe)

"It is the Tree of Life to them that hold fast to it..."; "...one generation shall laud Thy words to another, and shall declare Thy mighty acts..."; "...He that walketh *uprightly*... walketh securely..."

Surely Herr Himmelreich would know where I could find the old man who, lame as he was, had marched with the rest in the Procession of the Holy Scrolls, whose years went well beyond those of the Sofer, the Shamos and all the others of the congregation whom I had met. I clasped the Sofer's hand and thanked him for his time.

In the subdued light of the late afternoon with the vapors again descending, the road was scarcely visible. The mountains loomed black on all sides, the valley was still and as the sun grew even more distant, the temperature dipped lower. Yet I scarcely felt the chill as I came upon the orchards and grounds where the old man lived with his four children and their families.

He was standing at the door awaiting my arrival. Lifting his hand in greeting, he reached for his cane and started down the path to meet me. "It is indeed an honor to greet you, Herr Cantor! What great kindness brings you here to visit with us? Please come inside and meet my beloved family!"

Sons, daughters and grandchildren gathered around to shake my hand. I was quickly ushered inside where the old man motioned for me to be seated at the head of a table laden with sandwiches, fruit and pastries. One of the granddaughters, a comely girl with flushed cheeks and a slow smile, brought forth the tea; in no time I felt at home.

"You give me too much credit," I declared as we started out for evening service, "for I have come here not wholly without reason. I have brought with me a question that concerns me a great deal—that in fact occupies almost my every waking thought ever since I arrived."

"Ah so!" chuckled the old man. His comely granddaughter, obviously his favorite, had lingered behind to walk with them. Now he motioned to her to go ahead with the rest. "A man without a question, he is like a husband without a wife. A Jew without Torah—and a man without reason—" he tapped his leg with his cane, "—he is a lame fool, eh? 'Where there is no Torah, there are no manners and without manners there is no Torah; where there is no wisdom, there is no piety, and without piety there can be no wisdom. Where there is no knowledge, there is no understanding and without understanding...' Now what troubles you that a lame old man like myself could answer and account for?"

Quickly I stated my dilemma. "So you see," I concluded, "I cannot stay here in Bad Ems if I am unacceptable to the people, and I cannot be acceptable to them if I am not first acceptable to myself in all that I do in the eyes of the Almighty Praised Be His Name."

"Young man, you have given me quite a responsibility," declared the old man. "You must stay," he declared with a thump of his cane. "Promise me this and I will tell you what you wish to know."

"Yes, yes," I exclaimed. "Of course!"

He laid a hand on my arm. "Promise me that when you are Cantor here, for you will be appointed if you wish—that you will always bow at that same spot, on the south side of the sanctuary six rows from the bimah when you come upon it with the Holy Scrolls."

"But of course," I responded. "I only ask for just reason."

"Then I pray that you will find it so," sighed the old man, "for I see that you are very discerning."

"How many years ago," he began," I don't know anymore, I've lost count. Maybe seven score or more... at that particular spot, six rows from the bimah on the south side of the sanctuary, sat the most prominent family in the congregation. I knew them well... Neuberg was their name. It was a large family, maybe ten brothers or so, and two sisters. So pretty they were—too pretty. Harumph!"

The old man cleared his throat loudly. "I almost married one of the granddaughters…" his voice trailed off.

"The family kept growing larger as the sons and daughters took wives and husbands and they started to build their own large families, and soon there was no longer enough room for all the male members to sit together in the same row. Even though they kept adding more seats, the family kept adding more members and soon the row almost extended to the sanctuary wall.

"Now it so happened that at that spot near the wall was a wooden beam protruding from the ceiling. Joshua Neuberg, the head of the family, was a strong-willed old man, I remember him well. As if that particular row of seats in the sanctuary had been God-given to the Neubergs, Old Man Neuberg refused to move any of his family to another row. So all the members of the congregation, in order to pass by the Neuberg family row, were forced to duck beneath the beam.

"Picture it!" chuckled the old man. "The whole congregation ducking beneath a beam, bowing their heads as they squeezed past the Neuberg family! What could they do? Joshua Neuberg had practically built the synagogue singlehanded. He was a pious Jew, a prominent burgher in Bad Ems. The Rabbi, the Shamos, the Cantor, everyone tried to persuade Herr Neuberg to divide the family into more than one row. But ahh, Neuberg, he was a stubborn man. A strong man and a good man, but a stubborn one."

"That granddaughter," declared the old man with a tap of his cane, "she was just like her grandfather: stubborn! Her father insisted that I move into the same house with the Neuberg family and take over a part of the family business and I refused. So?" His eyes twinkled as he gazed ahead on the path at his own granddaughter, "Well so, finally as happens in time, the people grew accustomed to the awkwardness of the situation and what was forced upon them by so prominent a family as the Neubergs. Automatically they would dip their heads and bow when they came upon this place on the south side of the sanctuary six rows from the bimah. And the boys, they all made sport of it. Yes, I remember it well!

"Then, fifty, sixty years ago, finally it happened. The Family Neuberg outgrew the row under any and all circumstances. There was simply no more room to seat all of them together.

"It would seem a simple matter to anyone but Herr Neuberg—or perhaps the people were not so simple after all. For indeed, it was they who had been forced to dip their heads and bow for Herr Neuberg; why should he not pay for that privilege? Why not enlarge the walls and rebuild the entire sanctuary to make room for the Neubergs to remain seated in a single row?

"And as you might have guessed," continued the old man, "that is exactly what happened. Herr Neuberg was easily persuaded to remove the beams, enlarge the walls and install twice as many seats in the sanctuary. Now the Neuberg family row extended from one side of the sanctuary to the other.

"With no more beams that had to be ducked under and plenty of room to march comfortably past the Family Neuberg—maybe it was a habit—the people were accustomed to dipping their heads and bowing at that place. Or maybe it was gratitude," he shrugged, "who knows? They continued to bow as they had always done, and the children bowed, and the children's children, even until this day, the descendents of the Neubergs still sit in the same row, and although they have long forgotten the reason why, every member of the congregation continues to bow as they come upon this place on the south side of the sanctuary six rows from the bimah."

Together we laughed long and hard. "But, tell me. It is so absurd, how can you let them continue to—"

The old man straightened and gripped my arm. "I?" he exclaimed, gazing up at me.

Then I remembered what I had promised him. As I lifted my eyes, I saw before me once again the great glass dome of the synagogue radiant against the setting sun now threading the skies with a fiery array of scarlet and purple and rose. God's universe mirroring the interior of the sanctuary.

Author's Note: This is a true story that originated with the late Cantor Hugo Chaim Adler. It was told to his son, Samuel Hans Adler, who related it to me. It was first published in 1968 by *Midstream.* Because it is his story, I dedicate it to Cantor Adler, my two daughters' "Opa," whom I and they never had the privilege of meeting.

YOM KIPPUR

David made a final check around the bedroom. Bertha was right. She wasn't helpless, she was perfectly able to take care of herself. And after all, he wasn't going to be gone that long. Yom Kippur morning services were only two hours and if they went longer he would...

"David!"

"I'm in here, in the bedroom."

"Do you like my robe?" He looked up, watching her in the mirror as she entered. "It's the new one, from the children!"

"Ahhh... yes. Yes, of course." David smiled at her reflection. "Yes, I like it very much. It's very—lovely." Yellow. Bright yellow. Too bright... and too fussy, with all that lace and the ruffles. She looked lost in it, especially now. She was so thin and pale... "There's tea on the warmer. And a can of soup—"

"Don't worry, all right?" Bertha grabbed hold of his hand, pressing it to her cheek. "I'll be fine, if you want to stay on, just call and—"

"No, no. I'll be back after the morning service." Her cheek was so warm and soft but her voice sounded unnatural, as if even though she was there in the room with him, she was talking to him from a distance. "And then maybe in the afternoon—if you feel like it, we can take a walk—"

"Good! A long one. I feel like it today. I feel so rested!" Bertha squeezed his hand tightly and together they walked through the living room to the door, their footsteps thumping softly on the carpet.

Outside it was still Indian Summer, maybe in the high 80s or even 90s. Sprinklers whirled on the apartment lawn and the large fenced-in play yard was already swarming with kids. One of the mothers glanced up as he passed by and smiled at him. He nodded politely and hurried on.

Since they'd moved here almost a year ago, he hadn't made a point of introducing himself to anyone. Even the neighbors across the hall were still strangers to him except for a nod and a few civilities when they met at the mailbox or coming and going in the hallway.

Maybe it was because he didn't want anyone to know about Bertha. He didn't like pity. Anyway, new friends at his age were absurd. It was hard enough remembering the names of people he already knew. Adding more to the list hardly seemed necessary.

Not Bertha. She was just the opposite. So outgoing... always listening to someone's story and keeping up with birthdays, anniversaries—her correspondence was staggering. She truly *cared* about others. If Bertha were well right now, she'd know everyone who lived in the entire apartment complex. But she wasn't. She wasn't well. She was ill. At least right now she was.

It would have been easy to blame everything on the move. A move was bound to disrupt. Maybe it was his fault. Maybe by his forcing it, by forcing the change... No. It was Time. Only Time could be blamed. The children were grown and had moved away... Keeping up a large house just for the two of them hardly made sense.

Change was just another circumstance, something to get used to, like illness. And next year—next year, again they'd be going to services together. Everything would be back to normal again.

Last night was the first time since they'd been married that they'd missed the evening Kol Nidre service at Beth Shalom and although they'd listened to it over the radio, David resolved he'd never do that again. The muffled responses of the congregation and voice of the rabbi settled like dust over the furniture. He could scarcely concentrate, yet he knew that was his fault and not the radio's. It was good that at least they could pretend to be there.

It was also his fault that he couldn't think of anything but—what? *What, what?* He repeated. That somehow he must convince her, convince himself of something so simplistic it had been long understood by both of them? That God was a just God and had not failed them after all? That all the weeks of testing, all the trips back and forth to the hospital... that in all of this "something that seemed to be right" was wrong—? *Wrong, wrong*, said his footsteps.

It was as if he'd become disconnected from who he really was or had always been, at least since his marriage to Bertha. Now he was moving through another time and space where everything that was familiar seemed to have run out through the holes, large gaps where he would discover himself sitting and staring at nothing in particular. *Where had he just been, and where was he headed? What would it be like without...*

He would come to in the middle of a conversation, aware that someone was talking to him—looking at them as if *what?* One day hope, the next day, despair; a desperate rhythm, the same refrain.

Wrong, wrong, said the voice. And still no sense. Scraps and particles of conversation fluttered by... he'd hear them all right and they'd seem real enough, yet they refused to make sense. So far away they were, and so—irrelevant.

Yet there were times when the transfusions took hold and everything was back, like last night. Smiling and radiant, propped up on the sofa, her short gray hair neatly framing her face... she was so beautiful, like a queen, dressed in a flowered dress she'd sewn from the silk they'd brought back from Japan three years ago. He remembered watching her smooth out the pattern, pinning on each piece—how clever she was, and bright. A Phi Beta Kappa at Vassar, and then on to law school. Clever, bright and disciplined. Raising a family of four children and maintaining a full-time practice...

Seated there, the darkness slowly spreading, he realized how lucky he'd been, and still was...

They only lived four blocks from the temple and whenever they could they walked. They enjoyed the leisurely stroll past the large estates, past the street that for thirty years had been their own. When they gave up the house for the apartment, they'd moved only a few blocks away.

As he reached the corner and turned onto the main thoroughfare, David was aware that something was different from the last time he'd been here with Bertha. Six months ago already, since she'd taken ill. Was something new, or missing? It was the sidewalk.

Stretching out in front of him and already sweating in the hot morning sun was a long black strip of tarmac. After all these years they'd finally repaved it. All those crumbly old slabs covered over! In less than a day no doubt; no doubt, only a few hours it had taken to pour it on and roll it out.

He swallowed hard, the hot tar fumes burning his nostrils. It reminded him of the time they'd re-carpeted the temple, the first time he'd stepped inside. Crimson, of all colors! *Gushing from all the arteries, the brilliant red...* yet now it seemed so natural, as if it had always been there—fitting, in fact. And—yes, even splendid. "Noble" was the word someone used when describing the sanctuary.

All it took to make everything all right again was acceptance. A simple conditioning; something new or changed that you finally got accustomed to. Soon he would be home again. The service was only two hours and two hours was nothing compared to a lifetime of being together. You could roll out pavement or a piece of carpeting in two hours.

What had possessed him to start out this morning without her? What selfishness, on this of all days! Yom Kippur, the one time of year... On this day, the rabbis said, there is no sadness, only joy at keeping a commandment.

Remember the Psalmist: "Serve the Lord with fear, and rejoice with trembling"... On this day more than any other, man must be joined with his brothers, his fellow worshippers. He must be part of a congregation. Two men raising their voices are more apt to be heard than if each should cry out separately.

The pavement was soft beneath his feet as it flowed ahead of him, dazzling in the sun. At a certain point it seemed to converge and disappear. Like water, like air—nothing but a silvery streak. Once there, now gone...

She was lucky, Sid said. Sid was a good friend, but a doctor first. He wouldn't deceive them. There were symptoms, and of course everything had to be checked. Various types and degrees of this particular disease...

Types and degrees! How naïve should he be? *There was only one*—one God! One body system, and if it failed... there were always transfusions, Sid said. First it was one every two months, then once a month. They'd called in the specialists: Boston, San Francisco, and now a man in Chicago... more research, new findings and many new alternative therapies as well. Even though her case was rare they mustn't give up hope...

If only he could cry and just once, let go. It was hot. His legs ached. Too hot to walk, with the sun so bright... maybe if he sat down for a minute and rested... There used to be benches here but they took them away long ago when the city buses went.

No more buses here and no reason even for repaving the walk. Probably cheaper than ripping it out. Just like anything. Once established, it was hard to re-do, even though no one walked anymore. How many years was it since the buses had left? The houses were already considered old and the neighborhood settled. He could still remember the day they moved in. Right after the High Holydays. It was raining and temperatures were already falling... the house was finished but the lawn wasn't in yet...

Fifty years! If only he could cry. Basements poured and boards going up, just skeletons. And then the walls, windowless... each week something new; each day something different.

You never know what to expect. Then one day you wake up and no one's there anymore. All the workers are inside; out to in. Everything hidden from sight so you'd have to guess how they were progressing. You never knew what colors they chose for the walls and how they furnished it.

Uncertainty was always that way. You never knew but you were still called on to accept without knowing.

The mounds of dirt were finally rolled out and seeded. Perfect lawns, little green sprouts in a matter of weeks. Then all those trees they'd planted, how scraggly they were. Like the kids and now the grandkids in kindergarten and first grade... amazing, how fast they grew.

In that brown house was a fire once. He remembered the photos in the newspaper, the house in flames... when was it? And the insert in the bottom corner, a blurred photo. Tommy was his name. Six years old. By the weekend a wire fence went up, the house roofless and gutted. Then in less than a year, it was better than new. Yes, it could happen. *It could reverse.* It didn't have to be wrong or negative. *It could be good and we could go on from here as if nothing had happened.*

The new owners had placed flower boxes on every window, and awnings. Cheerful geraniums and red-and-white striped awnings. Red was bright. And startling. Red flowers. Red blood.

Number 391 was always for sale; it was for sale again. How many times? Whoever moved in never seemed to stay. Nothing is permanent. Every time it was sold it was painted a different color. Now it was yellow. The house next door was never for sale. It was ugly, with no flowers anywhere, and no gardens. Always the same dull gray with untrimmed bushes.

The problem was, it was all too perfect, the way people said it never should have been. They said there should be quarrels and separations. And today even, people who were married for as long as 25—30—40 years, got divorced. Two people married that long are supposed to find faults.

No. Never. He loved everything about Bertha and always had. And besides love, there was respect. They'd had a perfect life. Enough money, no struggle. Bertha had retired from a brilliant career as an attorney and he'd done just as well in business. All three kids had been well educated, they were healthy and happily married. And rooted. Jewish homes, Jewish families...

A little boy munching on a cookie toddled down the drive and pointed a pudgy finger at a bright red chrysanthemum. "Red?" he asked, the crumbs rolling off his chin. "Red?" he repeated.

David smiled at him. Joey's age, he must have been. Or maybe Jonathan—he could never keep all the grandchildren straight—six of them, and another one on the way! God is good.

Strange, how much one learned just in passing by. Each home and the occupants... how much in the tiny span of a life. Even one's own children—appearance maybe, and habits that became familiar. Little things that congealed, creating a style or manner that one came to expect.

Soon even the smallest gesture could be recognized: the way she buttered her bread, methodically starting at the center and working out toward the edges, lips pursed, fingers taut on the knife; cutting it in two's and fours for the children, trimming off the crusts ("You'll spoil them," he teased).

Baking the challa for Shabbat. How they loved it! Gathering in the kitchen, fascinated as they watched her braid the dough, then braiding their own mini-challas. Stretching and twisting, under and over, over and under. Bertha's challa was so moist and fluffy it looked and felt like cake and tasted even better.

The way she shined her shoes. A ritual, before she went anywhere. Neatly lining them up beneath her dress; jewelry, gloves, purse, everything would match. Books she was reading, neatly marked with paper strips. Slowly, methodically she'd work through the books. They might have been started months, years ago, but they'd be finished. She was determined all right. Determined to do everything right, and for everyone else.... especially for him.

She was the one who'd said he must go. *Go on as if nothing's wrong. It's the only way.*

Maybe if there could be someone to talk to. Friends; they had enough of them. "That's what we're here for," they'd say. No. Not even friends. They'd never understand.

He could have gone to the rabbi. No. Never. He was too young. Young enough to be his son. And then if he did go, what would he say? Seated in one of those modern uncomfortable chairs, phones buzzing, lights flashing... did he really think he could talk to that bar mitzvah boy about Bertha's illness? Anyway, rabbis were not faith healers. They were human beings like everyone else. And like everyone else, all they could give would be words. He'd already had enough of those. Worn-out sentiments, threadbare litanies, knowing looks and sympathy. Greeting cards. Cheer and comfort.

"Chirrup, chirrup!" A robin landed in front of him and was joined by another. They flew away, chirping noisily. Soon it would be winter again and they would fly south. They would be gone.

Chirrup! Chirrup! It was hot. His legs were so weak. Just a few houses more. If he just kept going, if he could just forget about himself... if he could just forget...

It was a good day today. A very good day. This afternoon they would take a walk, rest a little first... Other congregants were streaming in from the parking lot. Strangers. All strangers. People moved and retired, no one he knew. And died. People died. Of course.

Of course they died. They lived and died. There would still be room in the sanctuary; he'd still find a seat. One seat. And the time would pass, he'd be home in no time. It was a good day. What were two hours? In the afternoon they'd take a walk...

At the entrance one of the members smiled and greeted him. Who was he? He'd seen him before but couldn't remember his name. Handing David a prayer book, he ushered him inside.

THE HOUSE WITH THE BLUE DOOR

Toni had just lowered the beaters into the egg whites and turned on the mixer when the doorbell rang. "Damn!"

When beating egg whites, one minute, one split second could be fatal and once started, the starting and stopping... she flicked off the beater switch.

"Pardon, I'm so sorry to intrude." In spite of the heat, the man on the other side of the screen door was wearing a suit and tie, the cuffs of his starched white shirt correctly prominent at the wrists. He was probably about her age, Toni thought, or a little older maybe, with clear blue eyes and thick reddish blond hair. Handsome, like Robert Redford or Paul Newman. Very handsome. And well-built. He spoke with a British accent, yet clearly English was not his native language. "My name is Henri Blau. I live across the street, that is, since yesterday. We just moved in."

"I'm sorry... I mean, welcome... I mean, I'm baking and my hands are sticky, I just—"

"Ahh, I hope I didn't—"

"Oh no, not at all," Toni lied, feeling the heat rise to her cheeks. While she was speaking she was aware that Mr. Blau's eyes had traveled downward, taking in all of her. And no wonder. She was practically naked. Dick was in Belgium on business until tomorrow, all three kids were away until September... After her morning shower she'd padded into her 17-year-old daughter Laura's room and snatched a discarded halter and pair of cut-offs from her closet.

Although at age 43 Toni could still fit into her size 6 wedding dress, Laura was a size smaller and the shorts were absurdly tight. The halter was only a scant piece of cloth, ample enough for Laura at age 17, but on her own exceedingly generous adult body, scarcely covering her nipples.

"I—it's too hot today. I really shouldn't be baking," Toni stammered.

"Oh, but I'm so sorry for interrupting you," he repeated. "Our water heater is broken and we still don't have phone service. My cell phone lost its charge—may I please—"

"Of course," she smiled, leading him into the family room and wondering if she should leave him there alone. Maybe she could dash upstairs and change her clothes, or at least throw on a blouse over the halter. She wasn't accustomed to greeting strangers practically naked. Maybe she should just wait until he was finished making the call. *How did she really know he was the new neighbor?*

Disgusted with her silly sense of distrust, angrily Toni padded back to the kitchen and re-inserted the beater in the bowl of egg whites. In spite of the interruption, the egg whites fluffed up over the sides of the bowl and formed a perfect foam.

A burglar, Toni reasoned, would have already gagged or shot her. Or at least knocked her out. And if he was a sex pervert or serial killer, by now he would have raped her.

With her olive-colored skin, long dark hair and large green eyes, Dick liked to tease that she was a cross between Sophia Loren and Mona Lisa. She knew she was attractive and at least ten years younger looking than her actual age.

"Not many women today do their own baking," remarked Henri, coming up behind her.

"Yes, I suppose that's true." Toni plunged her hands into the dishpan of soapy water, turned and grinned defiantly at him as she reached for the towel. "So your name is Blau. We've always called your place 'The House with the Blue Door' because of the, well, because of its blue door. What a coincidence!"

"Yes—oh yes—the door," smiled Henri. "I hadn't thought about that. Yes, it is blue, isn't it?"

"We have three showers," said Toni. And of course a washer and dryer, in case you need it. Sometimes the plumbers promise to come, as you know, and—but I do hope they will—I mean, I hope it won't be necessary to—"

"Yes," said Henri. "Thank you. You are very generous."

"And I do hope you have no more problems. But if there's anything else—and—I would like to bring you some cake if I may," Toni added impulsively. "When it's baked—it's been a long time since we've had a new neighbor, that house has been vacant for over two years—and do feel free to use our phone until yours is installed, or until your charger is—or until your phone is charged. And if there's anything else—?"

"Thank you," said Henri.

Toni closed her eyes, leaned against the door and felt sick. Why, why, why had she offered to bring them some cake, she wondered. When it was so beastly hot, the kitchen was already unbearable and with the oven on, even worse. She had been resenting today's baking project, but it was one of those times when she knew she had no choice. Tomorrow was Roslyn Martin's birthday. Roslyn's husband, Ronald was one of Dick's law partners. It was Toni and Dick's turn to do the birthday party thing and invite the other two partners and their wives for dinner.

One could certainly never serve a store bought cake for Roslyn's birthday. The Martins were connoisseurs of good food and fine wine and Roslyn was a gourmet cook who had taken special lessons in Switzerland. They ordered their caviar and shallots directly from France and their curry from some godforsaken place in Punjab. Ronald could even detect pre-ground pepper or—God forbid! —anything that had not been authentically squeezed, shredded, pounded and worked on in all those tedious time-consuming procedures that were Napoleonic Code for any gourmandize.

One couldn't just take over a few slices of cake to a new neighbor. Probably they would have children, a large family if they bought a house that size. Six bedrooms, seven or eight baths…. another cake was in order.

Why was she shaking? She felt giddy inside, like a teenager.

Not only another cake, but probably a trip to the store for more eggs. Toni stared down at her bare feet, at the ten freshly polished toenails. They were the same shade as the lipstick and nail polish she would wear tomorrow.

Maybe she really did resemble Margaret Browder, the protagonist in that novel she was reading. Margaret was a 40-year-old frustrated, bored and depressed housewife who had taken a triple-digit corporate job six years ago when her children were still young. Now she was doing it all and having a ball. She, Toni Pearson was a 43-year-old stay at home housewife with a law degree from Yale.

The Martins were dull and foolish people unless they talked about Polynesian poi poi, and the Andersons were just as boring because they never talked. She was sick of spending time with them. Sick of baking cakes and making parties, and—she stopped, catching herself before it slipped out. Sick of what, really? What *was* she sick of?

At age 43, you certainly do not feel frustrated, bored, depressed and unfulfilled, she chided herself. She loved Dick and their children and had never resented having to be financially dependent on someone else. She knew she was more than qualified to hold down a good position with a prestigious law firm. Yes, she certainly could have chosen the same lifestyle as Margaret Browder and even then, obligations like Roslyn Martin's birthday party would not have gone away. In fact, there'd be *more* obligations with two careers, and less time to deal with them.

Also, unlike Margaret, Toni would never have denied herself the privilege of staying at home and raising her children. She was fully aware that without a solid home base, without at least one parent available and open for communication 24/7, Laura, Bruce and Suzi may not have turned out as well as they had thus far. Dick, an international attorney, was gone most of the time in Europe and Asia.

In the novel, Margaret was sullen, resentful and—yes, she was jealous. Jealous of her husband Peter's professed relationships with other women, yet she was afraid to cross the marital line herself and engage in relationships with other men. For Margaret, breaking the marital taboo was too much for her to even fantasize about, until one day it happened. The reader travels with Margaret through one juicy escapade after another. Could sex get any better on page 51 than on page 48? Strangely enough, Margaret's and Peter's extra-marital affairs drew them even closer. They discovered a new intimacy in their marriage, a new freshness and excitement. They seemed to be more in love than ever.

No, she was not Margaret, Toni concluded. She was certainly not afraid she was missing out on life because she didn't indulge in affairs with other men—or women. Both were acceptable these days. The public was hungry for this trash. Reviews had been off the charts and the book already had a film option—which is why she'd snitched it off Laura's night table to take a peek at it herself.

Toni had to admit that some of the situations were remarkable—the fuck on the Ferris wheel in Prague was spectacular and so was the one in the Men's Room of the Sudbahnhof in Vienna with the two security guards gagged and locked up in the storage room. And the encounter with the nude lesbians in a lingerie store...

Good entertainment for bored housewives and curious teenagers, Toni decided. She, Toni Pearson, loved her husband deeply and passionately. Of course they had obligations. Like having children, they were part of any marriage.

Besides that, Dick was good in bed. She'd never felt the need to go shopping.

To her relief, Toni discovered she wouldn't have to go to the store after all. She had plenty of eggs, butter, milk and confectioner's sugar for the frosting... In ten minutes the second cake could be mixed, 35 minutes in the oven, clean up the kitchen, clean up herself, take a nice long shower...

This housewife certainly was not frustrated or bored, and certainly not blue... *blue*. The word parroted back at her as she headed for the bedroom to change her clothes. She paused in front of the full-length bedroom mirror and allowed herself to admire her slightly arched nose, well-formed mouth and flawless complexion. Her dark hair cascaded over her shoulders, framing her face with a tease of tiny ringlets.

Was it a curse to still be beautiful and so young looking, even at age 43? Of course not! Was Henri Blau aware that she wasn't wearing any panties beneath her skimpy cutouts?

Was there anything wrong with reading trashy novels?

Last night she'd fallen asleep in the middle of Margaret boarding a cruise ship for Hawaii where she would be meeting a male sex therapist and his female partner, who, Margaret had been told, would be punishing her for pretending to be faithful to her husband. For the punishment session, Margaret had been instructed to bring only a pair of black lace string panties and a mask.

Toni changed into a sleeveless flower print dress from Neiman-Marcus and tied back her hair with a scarf from Bloomingdales. From her jewelry case she chose her favorite heart-shaped diamond-studded earrings and matching bracelet from Tiffany's.

Who else but someone named Blau would have bought that house, thought Toni, crossing the street and starting up the cobblestone walk.

As she approached the blue door, Toni noted that it was old and cracked. In several places the paint was already peeling; one could see numerous scrapings and layers beneath. The flower beds on either side of the walk were overgrown with weeds that had choked off whatever remained of the perennials. The large cedars on the lawn had grown up over the front windows.

As she rang the bell she was struck by the notion that like Chinese nested boxes or Russian matryoshka dolls, one blue door would open to another blue door and another and another. She suppressed a giggle.

Henri Blau was standing there in the open doorway, still immaculately attired in suit and tie and looking more than ever like a cross between Robert Redford and Paul Newman.

For a moment he seemed surprised and a bit puzzled to see her standing there. Had he forgotten about the cake? Or maybe he didn't recognize her in a dress.

"Now it's my turn to apologize, isn't it?" Toni laughed. "I never introduced myself when you came over to use the phone! I'm Toni Pearson—the Pearsons, Dick and Toni from across the street—and here's the cake I promised!"

"Ahhh yes! Of course! And how beautiful. How kind of you!" Henri's jaw relaxed. He smiled graciously and ushered her inside. "Excuse me, I'll just put this in the kitchen."

Toni blinked and stared, blinked and stared again, her eyes widening with disbelief. The walls of the foyer and living room were covered with canvases depicting the same nude woman. Blonde and voluptuous, painted in almost every conceivable pose, the paintings were more than suggestive. They were lewd, graphic and disturbing in a sexually provocative way.

Henri returned. "Please be seated," gesturing toward the sofa. "Simone will be here in a few minutes. I'm happy to report that we have hot water, but only as of a half hour ago, and she is still dressing."

"I'm certainly glad they were prompt—or at least that they came—today, I mean," Toni stammered, seating herself on a cushiony sofa.

The paintings were intoxicating. As Toni continued to gaze at them—how could she not, since they were everywhere—she felt herself sinking into a delicious state of euphoria accompanied by a familiar aching sensation in her groin. She felt her nipples harden and her clitoris grow damp. The paintings were having an extraordinary affect on her, as if each of her sexual parts was being aroused simultaneously and she was willingly participating in a delicious orgy of licking and fondling and teasing and gently massaging to the point of orgasm. Then, just at the point of coming, it would stop and start all over again...

"When?" asked the Amazon on the wall opposite, grinning mischievously at her. Seated on a tiny red stool, her legs spread to an open 'V.' On her pubic bush a wreath of pink and yellow roses formed a circle around her large bright orange clitoris. Cradling the roses and forming a second wreath around her clitoris was a pair of bright blue hands.

Standing before her was the man named Henri. He had removed the lid from a crystal decanter on the coffee table. "Sherry?" he asked, picking up a wine glass.

"Thank you," Toni smiled gratefully.

From a distant room she could hear someone playing the piano, a Chopin polonaise that she played often herself but not so skillfully.

"Tell me," Henri's voice floated over the music, "you mentioned this house had been vacant for some time. Did you know the former owner?"

Toni jumped as the music stopped, followed by a loud *bang!* that sounded like the piano keyboard cover slammed down.

Clutching the sherry glass with both hands, Toni felt a sudden compulsion to squeeze it until it broke. How delicious it would have been to feel the amber fluid pouring out of the broken glass and onto her dress and legs; how excruciatingly painful to feel the broken glass cutting into her flesh.

"Not really," she replied in a voice that was surprisingly calm. "They—their children were older than ours and were already gone when we moved in."

"That is the American way, isn't it?" murmured Henri, lifting his glass and saluting her. His blue eyes were so engaging... "One rarely knows one's neighbors in this country. So I think we are already fortunate! But then, the pace of life here is so fast—so different from what we Europeans are accustomed to. And yes, in case you're wondering, these paintings are all Simone. And speaking of Simone—"

A long shadow appeared in the doorway followed by a tall bony-faced woman with straight brown hair and Dutch Boy bangs attired in a dun-colored chemise that hung shapeless over what seemed to be a mere skeleton of a body.

Toni had never encountered anyone so thin and fleshless. Her eyes were ringed with purplish gray bruises and they stared out at her from their shadowy craters. Her mouth and jaw line protruded beneath a tissue-thin layer of skin, giving her face a corpselike appearance. A cigarette in a long black holder dangled from the left corner of her mouth.

Puffing furiously, Simone glared first at Henri and then at Toni. Toni rose and held out her hand.

"So you are a pianist as well as a painter," Toni offered, withdrawing her hand when Simone made no effort to clasp it in greeting. She reseated herself on the sofa.

As Simone folded into the chair opposite, Toni had a glimpse of the large black oxford men's shoes she was wearing.

"I hate the piano, but Henri insists. He says it's good therapy."

"But you do paint," Toni insisted. "Do you have a gallery?"

"Gallery? Me? Ha ha!" Simone puffed furiously on her cigarette. "No no, my dear! I'm a writer! Didn't Henri tell you? Oh *Henri*!!"

"Simone is very successful. Far more successful than I'll ever be." Henri beamed at Simone, pouring a third glass of sherry and handing it to his wife. "Her books sell well and I keep telling her there's nothing to be ashamed of. They bring in much more money than I'll ever see with my work."

Toni shook her head. "I don't understand. I thought you said—"

"Oh dear!" Henri chuckled. "Forgive me for misleading you!" And before Toni knew what he was doing, he had leaned forward and impulsively covered her hand with his own, giving it a quick squeeze. "And now that Simone is here, I suppose we should get down to business, shouldn't we, Toni? May I call you Toni?"

Toni sucked in her breath and gently rocked the glass of amber fluid back and forth in her hands. She squeezed her legs together; her panties were already damp. "Yes," she said, keenly aware of the swell beneath Henri's trousers. "But I'm somewhat confused. Excuse me. If I recall correctly, it wasn't *you* who asked *me* to come over, but rather, it was *I* who—"

"Ahh yes, forgive me again! I forgot to tell you, Simone dear, Toni brought us a cake! I put it in the kitchen. It's lovely. Chocolate, isn't it? I think Simone lives on cigarettes and ink. Some cake would be good for you, darling. She never eats. She's too busy writing. I really should tell you a bit about her most recent novel because *she* certainly won't. It's already made the best seller list in France and Germany, and the English version is due to come out next month. Simone calls it trash. It's about a woman who lives in suburban Vienna and who—"

"They're all about women who live in suburbia," Simone broke in. "Bored, unfulfilled and usually brilliant women. Who else has the time to sit around and read novels? God. American women, how I hate them."

"Forgive her, Toni." Henri shook a finger at Simone. "You are so naughty, darling! You don't even know Toni. She is not like most American women!" Then to Toni: "Simone tends to—"

"To what? Tell the truth?" Simone broke in. "I don't *have* to know you, my dear! If it hadn't been for your husband, Richard—if Richard hadn't suggested we get in touch with the realtor to consider buying this house—"

Toni snapped out of her daze and bolted upright. "You know my husband, Dick—Richard?" she blinked.

"Why yes," smiled Henri, "we met him on the Riviera, when was it, a few months ago, wasn't it, Simone? He was with a charming woman, I forgot her name, Marie-Louise, was it? Or Jeanne-Louise?"

"Of course you remember her name, Henri! They were so sweet together, so much in love. He had just purchased an exquisite diamond necklace for Marie-Louise and I remember you admiring it. Dickie suggested that you, Ms. —

"Toni."

"Toni might be interested in working with Henri. He felt it might be good for you to get out a little. He said you'd been so cooped up raising the children and doing housework, baking and enter-taining... Anyway, back to my book. It's trash. I wrote it in six weeks. But it sells. It pays the bills. It paid for that fucking Steinway Henri insisted we get. Which is the reason why we bought the house, of course. For the fucking Steinway and Henri's paintings. We had to find a place to put both of them. And for Henri, too, ha ha!"

"Your husband is indeed, a very discerning gentleman," said Henri. "He saw my work at one of the galleries in Paris and he's been following me ever since."

Toni stood up.

"Don't leave yet," cackled Simone. "At least not until you hear what we would like to offer you."

"Yes, do sit down, my dear. Actually our water heater didn't break," apologized Henri. "Richard suggested the excuse, just to make sure you'd let me inside, to see how sexy you are. Of course, I didn't expect to find you attired in such an engaging costume—which was actually perfect! When you answered the door you looked more like a girl of seventeen—a *bon cherie* —than the wife of a famous international lawyer and mother of three children!

"But no," Henri continued, "that was certainly not what attracted me about you. Richard said, in addition to your beauty, you have an elegance and refinement that is rarely encountered among American women. They are either masculine or adolescent and so immature. Simone is a fifth generation Pennsylvania Dutchman. Ha! Ha! Don't worry, she knows I love her. She's a genius. She writes other books besides trash, but under a different name. She wouldn't tell you that. She's very modest."

Henri moved closer to Toni on the sofa. "And of course I was very drawn to you by the very fact that you seemed to find such charm in the simple connection between my name 'Blau' and the color of the door, blue. It showed a cleverness and sensitivity to those little nuances in life that most people disregard—and indeed often consider very foolish and somewhat precious. Although I must confess, I was not aware of this little pun until you mentioned it. Surely it must have been one of the reasons why, just as Dickie said, I was attracted to this house—and attracted to you—!— Not because you are blue, ha-ha—but because you are so sexy."

"Thank you," murmured Toni, pressing a hand against her burning cheeks. "Actually I thought it was a rather stupid thing to say, but at the moment I was so—so—"

"Ahh, but it was brilliant. You are brilliant and I knew that!" Henri beamed. "When I first set eyes on you, when I first crossed the street and walked up to your door, when I first—."

A faint yet insistent ring was coming from somewhere in the vicinity of the front door. Toni opened her eyes, the book falling to the floor. Quickly she slipped into her flip-flops, straightened her hair and went to answer it.

"Forgive me again," Henri Blau had changed from a suit to a short-sleeved jersey and Bermuda shorts. His forehead and upper lip were beaded with perspiration; he was noticeably distraught. "The repair people haven't come yet, and I'm afraid I'll have to make another call. If you don't mind—."

INGENUE

When the call came, I was baking bread.

"Hi Shelley, this is Charlotte."

Charlotte.

"Well hi," I cradled the phone on my shoulder, punched down the dough and rolled it over for another punch. *Did I know any Charlottes?*

"How *are* you, Shelley?"

"Why I'm just fine, I'm just—"

"You do remember me, of course! I'm dying to see you again after all these years! Would you be able to meet me at the airport next Tuesday? I have a stop-over on my way to New York, the Big Apple, you know!"

"The Big Apple," I echoed. "Yes, it's just down the road a bit, about an hour from here by jet."

Charlotte Fisher née Wainwright, she informed me somewhere in the conversation, was arriving on the 11AM flight from Columbus.

I brushed off the cobwebs from my memory. Ahh yes. Charlotte, one of my four freshman under-graduate roommates. How could I have ever forgotten?

When tall willowy Charlotte Fisher floated down the escalator and into my life again at baggage pick-up, I was struck first by the fact that in spite of what science tells us, nothing ever really changes.

Accompanying her were four smaller versions, 2-F's and 2-M's. "It's like old times!" she suggested, embracing me.

"Yes, I replied, watching the oldest child poke his finger into the eye of his brother. The youngest, still a toddler, had jumped onto the baggage carousel and was running as fast as her fat little legs could carry her toward the tunnel where the baggage would be emerging.

"Dorcas!" Charlotte raced toward the toddler, her large hoop earrings swinging wildly.

It was amazing that such a small creature could be the receptacle for the sound that emerged as soon as the security guard snatched her up by her diapered fanny just before she was about to disap-pear into the tunnel. "Keep yer kids off the belt," he barked, tossing her into Charlotte's arms.

For several seconds we stood side by side listening to Dorcas's shrieks. They were truly life-threatening. Meanwhile, Charlotte #3 had opened her back pack and dumped all of its contents onto the floor. Rubber balls, jacks, playing cards, coloring books and crayons, Barbie & Ken and a whole wardrobe of hats, shoes, bikinis, etc., were rapidly disappearing among baggage carts and the flurry of passengers rushing to claim their suitcases, wheel chairs, strollers, etc.

"Cordelia, why on earth did you do that? Here. Tell Mama why you did such a terrible thing," coaxed Charlotte, falling to her knees.

"I couldn't help it, Mama. It just happened!" Joining her baby brother, Cordelia managed her own version of earsplitting screams.

Come," urged Charlotte, sweeping up a headless Ken and shoving him into Cordelia's suitcase. "Let's go some place where it's quiet so we can talk. Come, Archidamus! Bardoph! Cordelia, Dorcas!" I now remembered that Charlotte had been an English Lit major. During the year we roomed together, I'd written more than one paper for her on Shakespeare's tragedies and comedies.

I was introduced as an old friend. All four pairs of eyes stared up at me distrustfully. Never before had I felt more closely allied with a newly hired nanny or overused babysitter.

"Ice cream, children! Archidamus is a Skinner, Bardolph is a Hurlock," chattered Charlotte, "and Cordelia is a Gessell; no, Ilg. No, I mean Gessell AND Ilg. Do you know Auerbach?"

"Not personally," I smiled uncertainly at Dorcas as her tiny howling body toddled in front of us, leaving behind a trail of what was obviously not tears.

"You're probably still wondering why I bothered to look you up," continued Charlotte. "Goodness, do you make your own bread often? How good of you to meet our plane! What do you *do* with yourself all day?"

"Meet planes," I said, "and bake bread." I was relieved that Charlotte did not intend to pile the five of them into my four-door sedan sans infant seats. My own two children had already been dis-installed from Stage One Seat Regulations and my Toyota Camry comfortably seated four only. Charlotte was staying at one of the airport hotels and the van was already on its way to chauffer them door-to-door. I was instructed to meet her at the hotel coffee shop.

"You won't believe it, Shelley, but I'm liberated!" Charlotte shrilled as soon as the maitre d' seated all six of us. "I'm thinking of having my tubes tied and I've finally found the perfect au pair! She's arriving at Kennedy Airport from Iceland this weekend, which is why we're going to New York. We want to give her a Full Family welcome as soon as she steps onto American Ice, I mean Land. Travis, my husband, is meeting us there so we can do this all together. Bardolph, honey, stop picking your nose in public. You're old enough to try to be an adult once in a while. Smile, Archidamus. All of you can have chocolate if you like. Cordelia, the water, dear, do be careful. And Dorcas, take the menu out of your mouth. It's filthy with all kinds of flu germs. I'm dying to know what's been happening in your life, Shelley!"

"Well for one," I began, uncomfortably eyeing Cordelia's experiment with her water glass that was now teetering on the edge of the table, "My husband William is an engineer and I—"

"Excuse me, Mother," interrupted Archidamus. "I have not decided yet. I simply must decide."

"I want both, Mama, I know I can eat both!" shouted Bardolph, a short stubby Charlotte with a husky voice and two fanglike front teeth that would probably buy a new vehicle or yacht for some lucky orthodontist.

"Both of what, Jackass?" sniffed Archidamus, snatching his brother's menu away from him.

"If Bardolph has both, then I want both too!" Cordelia tore at Bardolph's menu, her water glass not quite toppling over.

"DRAWBERRY! DRAWBERRY!" chanted Dorcas.

"Mama, would you tell that lady to stop kicking me? That hurts!"

"Shelley, dear," sighed Charlotte, "...please, would you mind not kicking Bardolph. Anyway, dear, you are old enough now to kick back, without relying on your mother to defend you all the time. MISS! WAITRESS! WE'RE READY OVER HERE!"

Archidamus, seated next to me and opposite Bardolph, grinned malevolently as he delivered another swift kick under the table to his brother.

"OWWWWWWwwwww!" howled Bardolph.

"Travis and I believe in cafeteria feeding until the children are old enough," Charlotte continued.

A heavyset waitress poking her hairpiece into a falling bun labored over to the table.

"Now," smiled Charlotte. "We'll have one pistachio ice cream sundae with—"

"DRAWBERRY! DRAWBERRY!"

"Cordelia, make up your mind, dear. It's the first lesson in life, isn't it, Shelley? Decisiveness."

"I'll start," declared Bardolph, the howling abruptly coming to an end. "I'll have a fudge marble sundae with butterscotch topping and pecans instead of walnuts, and royal cream peppamint—"

"Sorry, we only got vanilla." The waitress, whose name tag identified her as "Marble," rummaged in her uniform pocket for another hairpin.

Charlotte was losing it. "Then just give us five banana splits with—"

"Sorry, we got no more bananas."

"Aw gee, Mom. What kind of joint *is* this anyway?" pouted Archidamus.

"Disgusting," Bardolph added. "Yeah. Gee," sniffed Cordelia.

"All of you SHUT UP!" shouted Charlotte just as Cordelia's water glass arrived on my lap.

"Oh Shelley, I'm terribly sorry. Here, dear, use my napkin. Cordelia, I told you not to spill that water, dear. Don't worry, Shelley. Don't worry about anything, dear."

"Everything's fine now, Charlotte," I reassured her. "Most of the water landed in my shoes and I can easily empty them out."

"Now where were we?" Charlotte snatched away my purse from Dorcas and pulled Cordelia's fingers from the sugar bowl.

"Travis. You said that Travis..."

"Yes. Travis is a microbiologist. He isolates germs of some foreign species that believe it or not, only *he* knows about. But his main work is with fire ants, I mean predators of fire ants. Phorid flies. I think it's worthy of a Nobel prize. In September the children will be in school except for Dorcas and with the new au pair coming from Iceland... Cordelia, you're old enough to eat your ice cream with a spoon instead of your fingers. Here, Dorcas dear, let Mommy cut up your ice cream so you can—"

"NO, NOOO, NOOOO! STOP IT!"

"Mama, there's something black in my ice cream."

"What I mean is, how did you manage to have children and a career at the same time? How many books *have* you published? I just saw the latest one advertised on Amazon. How long did it take you to write it? I've been at loose ends for years. I'm literally green with envy."

"Pistachio?" I inquired, looking down at my dish of vanilla ice cream and double-checking the color. "I thought she said—."

"Mama—"

"My dear, how many books *have* you published? And I read that one of your novels is being made into a movie... how exciting! Here dear, not the whole scoop at once. Here, let Mommy... I always said I wanted to be in one of your novels. What I want to know is, how do you do it all?"

"Mama, whatever it is that's in my ice cream is dead and it's—"

"Don't tell me, I know all the answers," Charlotte groaned, pulling out a strand of hair from her mouth and snatching up my dish of ice cream, spooning it into Dorcas's open mouth. "Discipline," she sighed, placing the empty dish on the table. "Just discipline yourself and learn how not to sleep. Plenty of black coffee. Wipe your nose, Bardolph... I can't *stand* runny noses, can you, Shelley? Or black coffee. I have to have cream in mine. How do you put three meals on the table in front of five hungry mouths and keep the noses and table wiped, the cupboards made and the beds full? Impossible."

Archidamus belched.

"A woman is a slave to herself and her family. And to the rest of those invisible obligations that rise up all over the place. And then the birthday parties. Invitations that simply have to be answered, and usually with presents that have to be shopped for." Charlotte thrust her arms histrionically in the air and accidentally swatted Dorcas, who let out one of her baggage claim wails. This promptly set off Cordelia, Bardolph and Archidamus.

The concert was unbelievable except that it was real.

"There I go again," wailed Charlotte, joining in from underneath the table where she was mopping the floor with whatever had the capacity to blot, from the contents of our purses. "We've been together again for such a short time, Shelley, and I've managed to spill out my entire feminine mystique. I'm hopeless, I tell you!"

I left Charlotte thrashing on the floor looking somewhat like a seal with her large hoop earrings doing loop-like revolutions as she flopped from one puddle to the next in the avalanche of water that was now pouring out from above as the rest of the children decided to get in on the act. She was still discoursing on women's lack of adjustment to, I believe, meanings, or [mean] focal points or lack thereof, and creative energies that are supposed to be and are not, in relation to the suppression of the id. Or was it the ego?

After paying the cashier for the entire disaster, I waved good-bye, my hand pausing mid-air as if it had been frozen in the omniscient lens of some overhead camera. *Good-bye, good-bye!* There they were, a watery image secured to the pages of my virtual album: Charlotte in the midst of her focal points, lifting her arms and cupping her palms just in time to receive Archidamus's flying mound of ice cream.

But there's more. On the return trip from New York with the au pair from Iceland now managing the children, Charlotte and Travis insisted on taking William and me to dinner at the airport hotel gourmet restaurant.

"So you're an etymologist," William began as soon the appetizers arrived.

Travis frowned at the shrimp ball that he'd just pronged with his fork. He set down his drink and eyed William darkly. "I am a microbiologist," he said, "and currently I'm studying the habits of Phoridae, which are predators of fire ants. The genus Pseudacteon, or ant-decapitating fly, of which 110 species have been documented, is a parasitoid of the ant in South America. Members of Pseudacteon reproduce by laying eggs in the thorax of the ant. The first instar larvae migrates to the head. The larvae develop by feeding on the hemolymph, muscle tissue, and nervous tissue in the head. After about two weeks, they cause the ant's head to fall off by releasing an enzyme that dissolves the membrane attaching the ant's head to its body."

I thought William was going to choke on his own shrimp balls. The conversation moved to a discussion of the sewage system in the Indus valley during the rainy season, microbial levels of food waste in some of America's wealthiest suburbs, aquifer pollution, the shortcomings of academic funding for Travis's research on fire ants, and the longcomings of the waiter with the check.

Once more, it should have been the end of Charlotte but sometimes even short stories seem to beg for just one more incident... one more "take-away"...

As soon as the Icelandic au pair had settled in, the phonecalls began. Charlotte confessed she was so glad she'd found me again.

"The trouble with women is that they can't follow through with anything real," Charlotte complained. "There's always some setback or disappointment, whether it's family or just Life in General."

"Such as...?" Putting Charlotte on speaker phone, I continued folding the laundry.

"Now take Travis, for example. He's really happy. Why? Because he's so involved. He's passionately in love with his fire ants. He goes around with that nauseating gleam of dedication in his eye. He's even beginning to *look* like a Desperate Search for Truth. Not that it isn't inspiring, Shelley. It is inspiring to the point of complete frustration. He's oblivious to anything except his ants. And they are by far the ugliest creatures in the entire world. Have you ever seen them under a microscope?

"And then there are the children. They are as ugly as the fire ants, all four of them. *Mean* ugly, behavior-wise, I mean. Of course I love all of them dearly, the way a mother is bound to. But it's so sad that they're human and mortal. Do you know what I mean? I mean, alive and vulnerable and always getting sick and they talk and fight and have to be washed and fed and *freaking coped with.* Travis doesn't get any back talk from his ants. No fuss, no trouble, those lovely little glass jars of headless ants simply sit there, dead and *totally behaved.*

"Shelley, I'm convinced that I'm happy. It's not even the rhetorical question that concerns me. It's just that I'm never happy in the *real* sense. Number one, I think I think too much. I'm too sensitive to be happy. I read too much into life that's not there and then I expect too much. You see, to tell the truth, I think I am unlike anybody else I've ever met, and that's a serious problem."

"Yes, that is a serious problem," I agreed, starting on William's socks and underwear.

"My mind tries to be Platonic while the rest of me, my libido, is definitely Aristotelian. I can't help it. I'm not convinced that Woman was placed on this earth to be just preoccupied with aggravation, menstrual periods and a menial job or an Alpha Male. A woman has to do something important with *herself* that's not male related."

I took a deep breath and waited for what I should have anticipated that day at the airport baggage claim. "More than anything else, Shelley, I have always wanted to be a writer."

"What sort of writing are you—?"

"—motivation," Charlotte continued. "Good or great? Anyone can be a Hemingway or a Faulkner or Andy Warhol or Ayn Rand. It's simply a matter of dynamism. And as far as style is concerned, I'm certainly no beginner. I would never have to look for the right one."

I started on the second basket of laundry and decided not to correct Charlotte about Andy Warhol, i.e., that he was a visual artist and not a writer.

"...I'm in that in-between stage, Shelley. I see myself sitting at my computer literally *molding* my material, as if the words were some sort of malleable organic substance, like bread dough, for example. Specifically croissants. I am aware that a Part of Me belongs with the utilization of that Certain Sense of Power—that cohesiveness of Spirit that comes from Structured *Experience* and from, yes... Form Itself!"

Before hanging up, Charlotte whispered into the phone, "I wonder how many people like myself struggle with the same creative urgency. Is there anything more lonely than the artist's estrangement?"

A couple weeks later she called to ask if I knew *personally*, any literary agents who would get her in the door of a major publisher with the novel she planned to write.

I was working on a new novel myself that required considerable research, so I hadn't realized that a couple months had passed since I'd last heard from Charlotte. Her next call, however, was inevitable. The chain link had been established. I was already familiar with the behaviors of aspiring writers.

"I've enrolled in an online course," she shrilled into the phone one snowy afternoon. "This week I'm working on Running Flashbacks, Structural Parallelograms, Anagrammatic Faux Pas and Lethean Fallacies. Shelley, can we work through the assignment together?"

We???

"The reception is so poor. Charlotte. I think there's a problem. Can I call you back in maybe a half hour? Or an hour?"

By that time I knew Charlotte would be off somewhere else, maybe having her hair or nails done.

"How do you feel about pseudonyms?" asked Charlotte a week later.

Shivering, I clutched the bath towel over my naked identity. She'd caught me in a dripping shower dash between Boy Scout Merit Day and a falling cake.

"—anonymity," Charlotte was saying. "Self-confidence is the architect of responsibility and inspiration is the cornerstone to…"

Then it happened. Surely it could have been only accidental that I bumped into Charlotte at the supermarket. I was too exposed in Frozen Foods, which was directly adjacent to Charlotte in Diapers, Candles & Air Fresheners. There was no way I could duck in time behind Breakfast Cereals & Syrups.

"We've moved!" she shrieked, descending on me. "Travis accepted a position at the University! I wanted to surprise you!"

Archidamus and Bardolph were industriously decomposing a pyramid of lime juice bottles and Cordelia was working up a green cleanser roux which she was finger-painting onto Charlotte's coat. Dorcas, still not toilet trained, was puddling down the aisle, leaving her own green slippery remains behind her.

"And guess what, Shelley? I'm breaking into print!"

I smiled uncertainly as I watched the pyramid of lime bottles wiggle deliciously near the bottom.

Still smiling and nodding, I fled in the wake of a thunderous crash.

"In the May issue of the *Online Clitter!* ezine column, "Children Get In My Hair," was an article titled "Through the Eye of a Needle." It described how Dorcas had swallowed a needle and upon Bardolph's suggestion, had then proceeded to ingest a considerable length of thread to see if the needle's eye would capture the thread and thus be retrieved by pulling on the thread, drawing the needle through the alimentary canal, larynx and throat as one would draw water from a well.

The concluding incident of the story was a trip to the E.R. for a stomach pumping, and the "moment of reversal" was the discovery that the needle actually had been threaded, AND… Surprise! Dorcas had also swallowed a thimble.

I called Charlotte immediately to congratulate her, but she had already flown to New York on a shopping trip. The new au pair, who was from Fiji, didn't speak any English.

In the supermarket I paused before the sour cream. The head next to me was dressed in a Logan green beret and it was muttering something about "beef stroganoff."

"Charlotte?" I ventured.

Her eyes were partially closed as she counted. "How many quarts make a pint, Shelley? Shelley! How ARE you?"

I tried not to look down as hastily she drew the flaps of her coat around her.

"I'm serving twelve," she explained, "and I have nine pounds of meat."

"Pints usually make quarts when there are enough of them," I murmured, staring at her stomach.

"Aescalus," read the announcement. "Nine pounds and three pints."

THE TRAIN

It was cool here because it was underground. To get on the train and go out to the tracks you had to walk up two flights of stairs. The stairs couldn't be seen from here. First you had to go through a long tunnel.

Russell had once been through the tunnel. It was somewhat complicated because of all the cut-offs, but he remembered there were signs once you went inside. Lots of signs. No problem. He wouldn't have any trouble getting on the right train.

His mouth was twitching. In the train store he studied the titles of about a hundred paperback books on a rack. Next to the stand were candy bars and soda pop. It was twitching furiously. Little jerks, like a grasshopper was inside, right beneath the skin.

He couldn't find a single reason for taking that train and bringing Ruby's body back. Edith could do it. God knew she could be trusted. Maybe Harold, her husband couldn't be trusted because Harold was an alcoholic, but Edith surely could be trusted. She made a point of telling you she could be trusted whenever she had a chance.

If Ruby had had her choice, Russell knew she would have wanted the heart attack at home. It was a mean trick. The only time in their married life that they'd been separated, and she had to go and die.

Nothing on that rack except cheap pulp. Playgirls and faceless men, the usual mysteries, how-to's and science fiction. Russell hated science fiction. He didn't care for any fiction, or books in general, for that matter. He never had time for them.

He never had time for himself; he was always busy. Yet when he looked back on the years, there didn't seem to be much to show for it except the kids of course. But that was Ruby's department, or at least she always said it was. Ruby was a good mother, the kids turned out all right.

Russell fingered his keys and some change in his pants pocket and stole a glance at the cashier, a large black-haired woman with lots of eyelashes and lipstick. She was wearing one of those lacy white see-through blouses without a brassiere, although you couldn't really see anything. She looked familiar, even if Russell knew he'd never seen her before. Maybe she was a certain type, the type that worked behind counters or in those so-called night spots.

She didn't seem bad. A little cheap, but maybe she had to be, to earn a living. He watched her take out her lipstick with a little mirror attached on the outside of the case. The lipstick was a dark purple color, the same color as her fingernails, which were long and sawed off at the end. Must have been at least three-quarters of an inch long, and sprayed with sequins. It made him sick to look at them.

He watched her run the tube first over the upper lip and then the lower one, stretching her mouth wide. She ran her right index finger over first the lower lip, then the upper one. It made him sick to think of all the stuff that must collect underneath those nails. Like underneath a bed where you couldn't get to it with the Hoover.

Ruby always said long fingernails were germ traps. Before he could look away, the cashier glanced up and caught him staring. Russell felt the blood rush to his face. *Damn!* He glared at the rack of paperbacks, his eyes boring into *Suck Me to Death but Undress Me First.*

What he needed now, what he really needed, was a cigarette. He was angry at himself. Angry at Ruby, because all he had to do was think about smoking a cigarette and he could hear her shrieking about cancer, lung poisoning, high blood pressure, heart attack, et cetera.

Ruby never smoked. She never drank either or did drugs. Ruby never did anything until her death yesterday.

"She's dead!"Edith shrieked over the phone. Edith shrieked the way Ruby did, only higher. Right into the eardrum. Last night he thought the phone would crack open. She was five years younger, 59, in prime health. So what difference did it make?

He needed a cigarette. He needed a drink. No, he needed nothing. He was acting like a child. As soon as Ruby was gone, as soon as she was out of sight he was acting like a horse just let out of a barn. *Hey Russell, what are you trying to prove, anyway?*

The train was already an hour late. Not that it made any difference. Once he had the tickets, Russell knew he was going, even if he had to wait all night. At this rate, he might have to.

Again he took out his wallet and studied the tickets. Identical, except that one was marked "To" and the other one "From," and of course the destinations were reversed.

He decided to move them from the bill section to the change section. They were safer there because the change compartment had a snap on it. They would be safer. Or maybe not safer but more convenient, easier to get to.

Although he might need some change for tipping and there was a chance of opening the change compartment and the tickets falling out. The change in his wallet was change he might not have in his pants pocket for tipping. Even though he had only one piece of luggage, a small overnight suitcase that would go right onto the train with him, he wouldn't have to tip anyone for that kind of help.

Not that he was in the habit of tipping anyone anyway—but there could always be an emergency, when a ready tip would come in handy.

In the suitcase which he didn't really need, since he wasn't planning to stay longer than to catch the next train back home with Ruby's body, was his lunch, or dinner, depending on when he felt like eating it.

Two sandwiches, one peanut butter and jelly and one tuna fish, an apple and a banana. No, just the sandwiches and apple. The banana was already black and spotty, so at the last minute he'd decided to toss it in the garbage. Did he remember to empty the pail before he left? All he needed when he got back to an empty house was the smell of rotting banana.

Although he'd never taken a train before, Russell had been here at the station quite a few times picking up or delivering Edith and Harold at least once a year. Then there was a school friend of Ruby's who came in from Wisconsin until she died. Once an uncle of Pete Dutchman's was coming in from Toronto. The train was early so he wasn't there in time, so the uncle cabbed all the way out to Dutchman's farmhouse forty-two miles from the depot.

Dutchman never spoke to him after that. Maybe he should have offered to pay at least half the cab fare, maybe that would have been the decent thing to do. But what would he have told Ruby about that missing money?

He could've flown to Pittsburgh to pick up Ruby. The kids always took a plane when they needed to go somewhere. They flew the way they did everything else, without thinking. Russell couldn't imagine getting up there in the sky with nothing but air underneath to hold you up. He knew he was old-fashioned and he hated himself for it.

You could get killed crossing the street. You could get struck by a bolt of lightning or eat something in a restaurant and get food poisoning. Even in the best restaurant. Or one day you might simply keel over, like Ruby did. Call it fate or whatever you want, God had His plans and there was no changing them. Still, thought Russell, rubbing his eyes with the back of his hand, you didn't have to help Him along.

He'd always meant to take a train and this time was as good as any other, even though it was a silly trip and a waste of money. There was nothing more he could do when he got to Pittsburgh except get back on the train again along with Edith and Harold and Ruby's Body and bring It home for the funeral.

Once Ruby was dead, Russell told himself firmly, she was dead, no matter *who* she was. Even if she was his wife.

A cold shiver trickled up his spine and back down again as Edith shrieked the news into his ear.

"My wife is dead," he'd repeated out loud, putting down the receiver and gazing in wonderment at the empty kitchen, at the electric mixer, blender, toaster and neat rows of vitamins and herbs.

In the back of his mind something told Russell if he didn't get on that train today, he might never get on any train. He didn't believe in the Train Revival, regardless of what they said, or how many trains they claimed were back and running again.

Anything that was, has been, Russell told himself. And it'll never come back. Not even trains. And if Rochester, New York was any example, trains were doomed, almost dead. The station was almost empty when he got there and it was still almost empty now, three hours later, except for the ticket agent, the cashier at the gift shop, and himself.

Not that he minded. He hated crowds of any kind and always made a point of avoiding them whenever possible. People with their pushing and shoving and their foul smells and loud noises had a bad effect on him. They made him dizzy and nauseous.

The train traveled from Rochester to Ashtabula, Ohio. There was a stop in Buffalo and another one in Erie, Pennsylvania. But according to the time table, neither of them was long enough to get off and get back on again.

Not that Russell wanted to get off once he was on. No, he would stay put all right! That's why he even packed some sandwiches. The dining car, if there was one, would be outrageously expensive and probably dirty. They always were, or at least so he'd heard. And there was supposed to be a Men's Room on every car. He hoped so. No point in taking a chance of traveling into another car and ending up somewhere else. It was enough to see that things went right in Ashtabula. Because in Ashtabula he would be taken off and hooked on to Pennsylvania while the rest of the cars went on to Ohio.

The first thing to do, Russell decided, once he was on the train, was to make damn sure he was in the right car. He would ask everyone that came through with a uniform on if this was the Pennsylvania connection.

At Erie, if the train was on schedule and it wouldn't be because it was already an hour late, he would have one sandwich. That is, if he could hold out that long. He was already getting hungry and the goddamned train was already almost an hour and a half late.

With all the excitement and packing, he'd forgotten to eat lunch. Now it was almost 3PM. Maybe he would eat half a sandwich in Buffalo, the peanut butter one, and the rest in Erie. Then what about something to drink? You couldn't drink train water. That much he knew. He should have taken a thermos of juice or coffee.

Maybe some vendors got on when the train stopped. But what if they sold drinks open, in paper cups? If it wasn't in a bottle or a sealed can, how could it be trusted?

"Never eat anything off the street," Ruby always warned the kids.

He certainly couldn't eat a peanut butter sandwich dry. Tuna fish, any fish was impossible without water at least. Which was better? Dying of thirst or food poisoning? Or just dying, period?

Poor Ruby. How would she know what he ate and drank from now on? No. Just because she wasn't here to keep an eye on him, he mustn't start acting like a child. Of course she was right. She'd been right 90 percent of the time and Russell damn well knew it. She'd taken good care of him, he hadn't been sick in years.

Although he never really felt particularly healthy. Maybe he should buy something here at the book and candy place and take it with him. It didn't look like they had anything to drink except soda, and it was three, four times the price it should have been.

Besides soda and the filthy paperbacks and magazines and drugs and cheap souvenirs, there was nothing worth buying. Not even a cigarette machine anymore in the station. The magazine place had cigarettes on the shelf behind the cashier.

Ruby wouldn't have had all these problems. She'd have had the whole damn thing worked out. She'd have packed a complete dinner, not just two stale sandwiches. She would have packed fried chicken or roast beef or maybe both, and potato salad and coleslaw, and homemade rolls and muffins... and a king-size thermos of coffee.

Ruby! Again he wiped his eyes. Ruby never had all these problems, she never worried about where the Ladies' Room was or whether there was one, and if Ruby was there, the train wouldn't have been late. There'd be no changing in Ashtabula. She'd have called up the central office and demanded to have a non-stop train direct from Rochester to Ashtabula.

Ruby couldn't tolerate delays of any kind, and she sure wouldn't have stood for this one. But if Ruby was here, Russell thought miserably, she wouldn't be dead, and he wouldn't be taking a train in the first place.

It was already three weeks since she'd left for Pittsburgh. Ruby wasn't afraid to fly. No sir! She'd saved up the money, hoarded from groceries, she'd informed him before he could ask. So what if it had to be Pittsburgh to visit a sister who gave her nothing but aggravation? No, Ruby didn't think of that. She thought only about the trip. Going somewhere. Well, she went somewhere all right.

Russell took out his handkerchief and blew his nose.

That train store lady wouldn't be bad looking if she didn't have on all that makeup and those false eyelashes. She could look like the centerfold of one of those girlie magazines. Only she was older of course.

Wilmy used to look like one of those girls before she got pregnant and started to have children. Blonde and busty with a sexy mole like Elizabeth Taylor on the side of her mouth. Wilmy and Roger flew all the time and thought nothing of it. Skiing, scuba diving... last year they'd gone to Africa to hunt boars. Or was it New Zealand?

Leave it to Wilmy. They already had three kids and another one on the way. Roger was in the liposuction business. He and Roger didn't get along and never had, right from the very beginning when Wilmy first brought him home for one of Ruby's pot roast dinners. Maybe it was because Roger acted like he had a chip on his shoulder, like he was better than anybody else. Secretly Russell thought the whole marriage came about because of Wilmy's breasts that she always wore half hanging out.

Roger had no religion either—not that he had much of any. But Ruby did. He used to say Ruby had enough religion for both of them. She believed in Jesus Christ and Mother Mary and all that Saint shit and she went to church regularly; Russell never went. And now look who got to die first!

He wished he wasn't so damned shy. So what, if he didn't buy anything? He couldn't buy any of that junk, it was a waste of money. He never would have come into this store three times already if the train was on time. And it was none of anyone's goddammed business whether or not he bought anything or went to church.

It was public territory. He had a right to look. *Look but don't touch.* For Chrissake, he was worse than a child. How many times had he slapped his own kids' hands for going into a store and fingering everything? Fingering candy bars and souvenir ash trays. A crying towel. "Cry on me," it said. "Souvenir of Rochester, New York." What would he do with a crying towel?

The towel was stamped with a portrait of Lord Rochester and the City Seal. Junk. A store full of junk.

In five minutes he would have been here at the station for more than two and a half hours. It was not only the goddamned train station that was rotten, the whole world was fucked up. What could he buy here? A cheap magazine? Cigarettes?

For Chrissake, if thinking was as bad as doing, he might as well get it over with.

Discipline. Self-control. That's what he had to have. Certain things in life, like pleasures for instance, that weren't really pleasures after all [name one], like candy for example. You thought they were good until after they were gone. [Try to name one pleasure besides candy that tastes like candy.] Certain things you had to accept in life, like death.

Russell gave the paperback rack a vicious twirl. *Chill: The Daring Story of Two Gay Horse Traders in a Siberian Labor Camp; Virgo: The Adventures of a Baldheaded Pimp;* and back again to the *Suck Me To Death* book.

He'd never had any hobbies except furniture making, or he might have found something over there in the magazine How-To section. Anything to keep his mind occupied. A quick glance told him that all the woodworking books were for beginners. Russell was already into cabinets and dining room sets.

Ruby had no hobbies at all, except herself and that goddamned house that was overcleaned. Or had been, until she left.

"You want to live like a pig?" Ruby would screech over the Hoover. Ruby had always been jealous of his woodworking. Maybe that was why it had become so important to him.

"It could be worse," he'd taunted her once. "It could be another woman." He'd really hated himself after that remark when he saw how he'd hurt her, how all at once as soon as he'd said it, her face got all glittery and purple. She looked at him like she was either going to cry or kill him. Ha! As if she really believed there could be another woman, or anyone, ever, but *her*, goddammit.

"No," he moaned, reaching for her as she grabbed him around the neck, practically strangling him, and bawling all over his clean shirt. The two of them must have looked like baboons the way they carried on. After that, followed by all the Usual Stuff, like it was a moment that couldn't be wasted.

––––––––––––––

It was so quiet here, almost like a church. If only he could pray. When he was a kid he always felt good when he prayed, but after awhile he outgrew it and it never came back again.

They were married in a Catholic church. Whichever church or religion it was made no difference to Russell. Ruby's folks and Ruby herself had insisted.

"Why not?" he'd said. That was the first big mistake, he realized later. The first giving in was the one that led to all the others. Although he'd put his foot down when Papa died and Ruby wanted Mama to come and live with them.

"Over my dead body," he shouted. And when he threatened to move out, Ruby got scared. Mama moved in three weeks later but she got sick and died three months later. Died of a broken heart, Ruby said. In truth she died of a sweet tooth. Mama loved candy and sweets. She was almost three hundred pounds when they trucked her off to the nursing home.

If he could pray maybe he would feel better. When he was a kid he really believed if he prayed he would be able to do anything he wanted. He could even become famous. Praying seemed to make him believe in himself—that he *could* do it if he put his mind to it. Do "what," he was never quite sure, but it didn't seem to matter. According to people in the know, they said it worked.

All that praying wore off eventually. It had to. It was like slapping a coat of paint on an unfinished board. After awhile it started to peel off and there you were again with all your doubts and problems.

He was nothing but a fucking piece of board already starting to rot from overexposure.

"Dear God," he began, "we didn't fight much and I tried to give her everything she wanted, we brought three kids into the world. So what if it wasn't perfect, those 41 years? No one knew Maggie was going to become a nun or that Tim was going to join the military and hang himself in basic training. Nothing's perfect. At least one of them is normal. That's more than a lot of folks end up with."

Mine, answered God. *It was my fault, because I created you.*

Russell jumped. From somewhere at the far end of the station was a loud bang like an explosion, followed by screeching and a deafening roar that chased itself round and around the station.

"*MINE!*" God shrieked.

"MINE!" Ruby shouted.

Russell closed his eyes and felt himself sinking. The roar was the whale and he was Jonah. It was after him, eating him up alive, taking his heart, his liver, his p—; it was terrible. When would it stop?

Abruptly it broke off and the station once more settled into stillness. He opened his eyes, for a moment displaced, and blinked several times. *Be calm*, he warned himself, *like nothing happened. It's the only way. Otherwise—*

In the magazine rack was a book of Louis XIV furniture making, but Ruby didn't like anything except American Colonial. "Colonial is American," said Ruby. "All the rest is cheap copies for people with money."

He really enjoyed furniture making. He liked all the sanding and fitting together of the pieces. He liked the different smells of the varnishes and the smells of the wood. He liked being alone down in the basement. The basement was his, except for Ruby's washer and dryer. It was the place where he could count on no one disturbing him.

The kids and Wilmy had never done anything with their hands. They were the new generation that didn't believe in using their hands except for writing checks and dialing repairmen to do what Russell could do better himself.

Like the time he painted the kitchen for half the cost of the estimate. So what if one of the cupboard doors got stuck and he got a little paint on one of the begonias? There were times, he thought, when he probably got more pleasure out of sanding down a piece of wood than doing his thing in bed with Ruby. And then, of course there was the beauty of the finished product. Wood didn't talk back.

Russell wondered if he would ever feel like making another table again, or even a cupboard. What would he do with it? Who would really appreciate it now that Ruby was gone? He wished he had to go to the Men's Room again but nothing down there was calling. And he sure wouldn't go back into *that* place unless he had to. The smell in there was indescribable. Well yes, it was describable.

The cashier was wearing cheap perfume or maybe it was expensive. Russell couldn't tell the difference except that it was heavy and he could smell it. It seemed to have lodged itself in his nostrils. Russell had made a point of never giving cologne or perfume to Ruby so she never wore it except for some occasional lilies-of-the-valley stuff that one of the kids had given her once for Mothers Day.

Ruby's smell and taste had gone long ago. How could she know the perfume had gone bad after awhile and smelled less like lilies-of-the-valley and more like furniture varnish? Little by little so she wouldn't miss it, Russell had poured it down the drain.

Then there was the lilac stuff. Bottled Highland Lilac. He'd had a hard time fighting that, since Rochester was the Lilac City. Ruby was a native and that said enough. Like all other natives, in May on Lilac Sunday, rain or snow, Russell was dragged through Highland Park to ooh and aah over the damn things while Ruby stopped at every bush sniffing like a dog.

On Lilac Sunday it was rumored that people came to Highland Park from all over the world and although there was certainly a variety of people there, the rumor sounded more like propaganda to Russell. He never saw many out-of-state license plates and he doubted if people would come farther than Olean or Weedsport just to see lilacs that grew just as good in your own back yard. He himself was from Utica where there were plenty of goddammed lilacs.

"If you've seen one goddamned bush you've seen 'em all," he used to say. Then Ruby would steer him over to the refreshment stand for some soft ice cream. She knew where his heart was, all right. Russell loved soft ice cream, even though it was bad for you. "Empty calories," Ruby used to lecture to the kids. "Nothing but junk food, poison sugar!" But Ruby loved soft ice cream too, and on Lilac Sunday she broke down. Ruby loved strawberry soft ice cream, although Russell preferred vanilla.

What a treat it was. They even made a grape flavor for Lilac Sunday, grape-purple for purple lilacs. He could go for a scoop of some soft ice cream right now, but Lilac Sunday and Ruby were already gone.

The place was totally deserted. Russell had forgotten how large it was. Or maybe because it was so empty. He liked the way his footsteps echoed when he walked. He liked the high ceilings and all the poles and arches. It was old-fashioned and terribly fancy. Built way back at the turn of the century when they took time to do things right. It was built before he was born. It must have been really something in the days when the trains used to roar in and out all the time, noisy with people coming and going. It must have been a regular circus with all the lights flashing and the loud speakers and porters dashing back and forth with baggage carts, dodging in and out of all the skirts of the fancy dressed-up ladies and men in coattails and hats.

Then with all those chandeliers lit up and the lacy curtains on the windows, like a palace it must have been.

Now it was a slum. Only one of the ticket windows had been unboarded and most of the glass in the chandeliers was broken. The floor had potholes and in a couple of places buckets had been placed to catch the drips from the ceiling.

If he lived here in this station he sure would know how to fix it up. He couldn't understand why they'd let it run down, or why they let people get away with marking up the walls. They were a mess.

He stopped in front of a cartoon of an automobile that was supposed to be a nude woman. The headlights were her tits done in pink and the fat rubbery wheels in front were her thighs. She was supposed to be squatting. It was a clever cartoon, Russell thought, hoisting up his pants and tightening his belt buckle. Why did his pants bag? How much weight had he lost in three weeks?

Since Ruby had left he hadn't sat down to a decent meal although he'd promised her he'd eat. Three weeks she'd been gone. Why did she have to go for so long? They both agreed it was a waste of money to go all that distance for less than a month, even though two weeks, two hours with Edith and Harold would be enough to kill anybody. Poor Ruby.

Edith was a pig, she even looked like one, with her snout nose. She looked like that nude car. Except that Edith was thin. Terribly thin, and nervous. Probably Edith married Harold just to have someone to fight with. She was the type that needed fights, and there was plenty to find fault with in

Harold. They were always having it out over the bottle. The bottle that could have bought fur coats and carpeting, new vacuum cleaners and so on.

Russell didn't want to think about it. It gave him a headache. He was getting a hunger headache anyway. Why hadn't he stopped for a hamburger? He'd settled on hamburgers and tuna fish last week after fourteen days of frozen pizza and egg rolls. In the days before health food, he could still remember Ruby's fresh apple pie. Or lemon meringue. The crust was always soggy, but who cared? It was sweet and tasted like something, which is more than he could say about all that wheat germ stuff.

"Is the crust as good as the last one?" she would ask, standing over him with a knife.

"Better, Ruby, much better," he would answer automatically, closing his eyes and holding out his plate for seconds. Ruby couldn't face the failure of a soggy crust [she couldn't face any failures] and it took a sharp knife to cut a soggy crust. So they were always better than the last one except when Edith came to visit. Then of course everything went wrong.

The meat was tough, the vegetables raw, the mashed potatoes too watery. Russell didn't care about the pie thing. He'd found a great place downtown that was famous for pies and he used to go there for lunch once or twice a week.

Poor Ruby. She was a good wife and it was all for him, all for his sake that she'd made so many sacrifices. She was saving him a lot of heartburn, she said. So the least he could do, Russell decided, was to get on a train and bring her body back.

What if the train was already so crowded there was no room for him to sit down? He would have to stand. The thought of standing all the way to Pittsburgh made his legs ache. He'd read articles lately and seen pictures on TV about the bad service. He should have known better.

He'd be lucky if he'd even find a place to eat his sandwiches, let alone standing room. He hated eating anything standing up, and when he was hungry he always got terribly thirsty. A dry peanut butter sandwich, or worse yet, tuna fish would drive him crazy.

He switched his suitcase to the other hand. It wasn't heavy. There was hardly anything in it. Besides the sandwiches and apple, just pajamas, toothbrush, flashlight and clean underwear and socks. He should have put it down somewhere; he didn't know why he was lugging it around the station, except that he couldn't just leave it standing somewhere. Anybody, even though his name was on it, could come along and pick it up.

He could have checked it in one of those lockers. No, he knew better than that. Just as the train came in and he went to take it out of the locker, the key might get stuck. Or he might lose the key. Knowing the state he was in, for all he knew he'd be in such a hurry to get on the train he might even forget altogether to take the suitcase out of the locker. These days he didn't trust himself.

He'd been too much alone and his memory seemed to be slipping. Even the grandkids had trouble understanding him, and he for sure couldn't make head or tail out of what *they* said half the time. But that was nothing new. Between all three of Wilmy's kids, even between Wilmy and Roger and himself there'd always been a gap. He knew what he was in their eyes.

Ruby was the one they looked up to, with her superior position at the Cleaner's. She'd sent the kids to college, or at last partly. Wilmy lasted one semester, Maggie did the nun thing as soon as she could, and Tim got his education and early death at boot camp. Ruby went to work at the Cleaner's as soon as the kids were halfway through grade school. Otherwise she would have gone crazy, she said. Then after she became one of the superintendants the work began to drive her crazy the way Russell knew it would.

She took it out on him, saying it wasn't the kids or work but him that was getting to her, because he'd never gotten anywhere and didn't seem to care whether or not he did. He didn't seem to care about anything, she would shriek. Or anyone.

Russell always said it wasn't true, though actually that led to some lying on his part because he knew he could never make her understand that he was happy being on the assembly line at the plant. He really didn't want to be a foreman, even though it might have meant more money which he doubted in the long run, by the time they took everything out.

There were times, yes, there *were* times when he knew he didn't care about anything in particular. And even though he was ashamed of himself—even though he felt guilty, there were times when he would have liked to stay all day in the basement without coming upstairs, and all night too. Eat and sleep when he wanted to, and let the whole goddamned world rot above him. It was rotting anyway, so he might as well enjoy himself making furniture down below.

He forgave Ruby when she went on one of her rampages. He forgave himself for being such a bastard and pretending he could live without her, and for the mind-slipping, he forgave himself for that too. It was natural in a time of shock and grief. But Russell was frankly beginning to wonder what would be left of him once the shock and grief wore off. Somewhere in the depths of himself he knew that during the last three weeks he'd been using Ruby's absence as an excuse for a lot of things.

Such as the way he'd left the house just now. Wastebaskets overflowing, carpets snowy with lint and crumbs; who was there to see it? Who would check on him? Wilmy was off to Switzerland, Maggie was in the nunnery and Tim was dead.

If Edith walked into the house looking the way it did right now, she would have been suspicious, thinking god knows what, with a mind like Edith's. The mess was actually an exhibition, he told himself. Just to prove to Edith and Harold that he was in a state of grief and shock maybe. At the last minute he'd stuffed everything, even the empty peanut butter jar, into the bathroom hamper.

He must have dozed off. He dreamed he was on a train and the porter was coming through with a large tray of ham and roast beef sandwiches and a steaming pot of coffee.

"Compliments of the Railway," he beamed.

"Where are we?" Russell sat up and rubbed his eyes. It was very dark. How long had he been asleep?

"We just passed Ashtabula, sir. Ham or roast beef?"

Ashtabula! He was almost there! What an easy trip—and he'd slept most of the way! Russell felt like laughing. He felt like crying.

Hungrily he eyed the large stack of meaty sandwiches. "I'll take both. One roast beef and one ham. No, make it two of each."

"Yes, sir," beamed the redcap. "Coffee?"

"Please." Ahh, such service. Such delicious sandwiches! And to think he was worried! Smiling happily to himself, Russell settled back in his seat, unfolded a large cloth monogrammed napkin and unwrapped the first sandwich. It was too good to be true, everything happening so smooth he could hardly believe it.

Hey! Russell lurched forward as the train squealed and braked to a stop.

"CLEVELAND, OHIO," droned the station master. "All passengers traveling to Cleveland, Ohio..." CLEVELAND??!!!

Russell jerked upright. The numbers on the large station clock flashed on and off as they moved one minute forward. Three-thirty-five. He'd really slept. How could he be so tired? Crazy dream, in the middle of the afternoon, no harm in dozing off... Why wasn't the coffin big enough? Leave it to Edith and Harold to try and save money on a coffin—as if it was *their money*!

Ruby wasn't a big person, she'd fit into a regular size coffin, so why did they try and get her into a child's size?

Angrily he eyed the tiny rectangular-shaped box and ran a hand over the lid. His hand was experienced. He knew good wood. His hand could feel a good finish.

What was this? Why hadn't he seen it before? *What was it?* He picked at it with his fingernail until at last it peeled off, uncovering a small round seal, a raised picture of an eagle with a flag in its mouth.

Where had he seen that eagle before? Of course! He should have known right off; it was Harold's company seal! The company he worked for that sold men's underwear!

The box wasn't a coffin after all, but one of Harold's cases, the kind he used when he went on the road with his underwear samples.

"Jesus Christ!" he exploded. "Couldn't you wait? Couldn't you wait until I got there?"

Russell gripped the handle of his suitcase and mopped his forehead. He was sweating terribly. He was drenched. Crazy dreams. The idea of Ruby folded up in one of Harold's underwear sample cases was really lunatic. He had to get hold of himself. Maybe he needed a little walk to exercise his legs.

It was so funny, the whole thing was so funny. Why did he suddenly feel like laughing? It was that lady car on the wall. The lady car was making him laugh.

"Fuck U," it said underneath in large gold letters. He hadn't noticed the lettering before. He'd once had a green car like that, with a long rear end. A Studebaker 4-door sedan with a radio.

Ruby loved that car. It broke down on the road one day coming back from the country, with six pecks of tomatoes on the back seat. The one thing Ruby always canned were tomatoes, although Russell didn't know why. He hated them. Maybe that was why. They cost twice as much to can than to buy on sale at the A & P.

The big tit headlights were really funny. Ruby had big tits and Wilma inherited them. He liked to press them together [not Wilma and Ruby, but Ruby's tits]. They were like two large Parkerhouse rolls. He liked to nuzzle his cheek against them and... With the help of a Pepsi Cola truck they'd managed to get the Studebaker to a service station down the road.

It was four o'clock. Two hours already he'd waited. Actually three, if you wanted to count the first hour of waiting before the train was due. In all his years of waiting for doctors, dentists, Ruby's hairdresser and veterinarians, in all his waitings for Ruby, this one was the worst. He should have driven. He'd have been halfway there now; he knew the roads.

He enjoyed driving. No. That was lunatic. How could he have fit Ruby's body and the coffin, plus Edith and Harold, into his Ford Focus?

If only that goddammed hammering would stop. Hammering that was coming from the basement, of all places! Who could be down in the basement but himself? Everyone knew the basement was off limits. It was forbidden territory to everyone but him and Ruby on laundry day.

Rat-a-tat-TAT. Rat-a-tat-TAT. Now a loud shriek followed by another, and another. What was she shrieking about this time, goddammit? When she raised her voice the whole neighborhood could hear.

Rat-a-tat-TAT. Rat-a-tat-TAT. Was she really inside, trying to get out?

He could feel the vibrations all the way through his body, he could feel it coming up through the floor, it was making his legs shake, his whole body was shaking. That damned eagle. Was he standing on top of it? Was the lid coming up and was he holding it down?

He had to get hold of himself. Of course it wasn't Ruby, and the eagle was only the company seal. It was the train! The train was shrieking and making all the vibrations, because the trains came in below, underneath the floor of the waiting room. A large train sure could shake up the whole damn place. But the shrieking—that was no train whistle! It was too human.

———————————————

This time when he awoke, the station seemed darker, although according to the station clock only ten minutes had passed. Unless the clock was broken. Everything else was broken. It seemed like longer than ten minutes. It seemed more like a whole night. He felt so rested. He was glad it was dark in here because the brightness would have made his eyes hurt. That happens when you're inside too long. Your eyes hurt, they start to water and sting.

It wasn't important to see everything. Sometimes it was better not to see at all, just like it was better not to know what time it was or whether the clock was actually broken. It sure made the waiting easier. Or maybe because he'd been waiting so long already, it didn't make any difference anymore how much longer.

Maybe that's what life was all about and maybe that was the thing about it that he never seemed to remember. That nothing really mattered after all, that you did your best, you tried to be happy, took the good with the bad... and if it was more bad than good, so what? What was a little pain? It passed. It would pass. Bright lights were a nuisance anyway. They caused too much pain.

Maybe the goddamned train had been cancelled. Maybe he'd slept around the clock and it was actually tomorrow. He could check at the ticket window again. But what good would that do? And after all, what difference did it make? Another hour or so, another day; he could wait.

He had whole years ahead of him to do nothing but wait. And he couldn't leave anyway; he was going to Pittsburgh on that train whenever it arrived, so why pester the ticket agent again? No point in pestering anyone about such a small thing as a train arrival. Anyway, how could the ticket agent tell him anything different this time, or tell him anything he hadn't told him before? Because the ticket agent was only a broken record. There was no man back there, only a machine. "Due any minute, due any minute," it squawked like a parrot.

No one was at the window and the room behind was also empty.

Russell peered between the bars. The office was dark. Poor fellow. Working all day with no one to talk to. He must get lonely, he must be tired. Who knows what kind of life he leads? Maybe his wife is dead or maybe no kids, nothing to look forward to when he comes home. Probably gets paid practically nothing for working here, and who knows what's wrong with him.

Something was wrong with practically everybody and that means doctor bills and other expenses. And with the price of food going up... maybe that poor man had to worry about blood pressure or ulcers, and special diets.

What does he need a son-of-a-bitch like himself pestering him about a late train—as if he could do something about it! Poor fellow. Let him rest, let him take a break. He didn't need people like Russell making his life more miserable than it already was.

That public phone over there was probably working. It would be easy to call. He could even have Edith and Harold paged if they were at the station. That would be easy enough to do.

He could see Edith's face, he could see her twitching mouth, her hate-filled eyes. And Harold, snickering up his sleeve; they'd never believe the train was late or maybe cancelled.

Edith would have gotten to the bottom of it. She got to the bottom of everything, like Ruby.

What the hell? What did he care what Edith thought—or what anyone thought, for that matter? Couldn't he live the way he wanted? Hell! Why not start today?

Why not start right now?

Russell straightened his shoulders and returned the stare of the man who was confronting him in the mirror of the Men's Room as he washed his hands. He shouldn't have waited this long to take a pee, it wasn't good for the bladder. The smell in here was not to be described. He remembered saying that once before, but no one heard it so it was worth repeating.

He should have worn another tie. Or pants that didn't bag so much. What day was it? When was the last time he'd picked up a newspaper? There must be a newspaper in this place, even though most newspapers weren't even being printed anymore. Yesterday's paper would do.

That was some cashier with those big tits. Like two big headlights underneath her see-through blouse.

"Hello there," said Russell. "I'd like just one cigarette, if you don't mind breaking open a pack for me and taking one out."

Was she really unbuttoning her blouse? This was no dream. No dream could be as good as this. Because now she was coming out from behind the counter, stark naked except for a pair of sparkly high-heeled shoes and a silver garter. She was holding up a pair of lacy black stockings.

What the hell, Russell decided, breathing heavily. *I don't have to go to Pittsburgh. I don't have to go anywhere.*

He rubbed his mouth. It hurt from all the grinning and twitching. He hadn't realized he was grinning until now, but he couldn't help it because she kept coming toward him and now she was screwing a large red stone into her naval.

Because it was enough, it was enough already, he didn't have to keep grinning. The stone was flashing like a traffic light.

"Red is for Stop," he whispered. "Here, take this first and then let me explain before you stop it. Let's start over again, please, and let me explain. You see..." Shakily he opened his wallet and searched for some change.

Where the hell was all his change? "I'm supposed to be taking a train to Ashtabula. Or at least at Ashtabula they change. They take off the end and send it to Cleveland."

"I can't," said the cashier. "If I do it fer one I'll have to do it fer all."

"No, not all," Russell insisted. "Just one, and just the end. I bet you thought I was going to Cleveland, didn't you? Well I'm not! I'm going to Pittsburgh! But you know, I got to thinking. I got to thinking, and you know, it's really pretty stupid, just to go and pick her up and come back. Let Edith do it. Edith can handle it, she can handle anything. Let her do the dirty work for a change."

"Even if it's dirty I can't open it," said the cashier. "It's either all or nothin.' It's against the law. Y'see this seal? I can't break it. I can't break no seals. But if you're willin' ta pay fer the whole pack—"

"Of course I'll pay for it," he declared, "but not the way you think. I won't be caught smoking the whole pack. Maybe somebody else, but not me. No sir! Wait a minute, Miss. Let me cash in my ticket for some change first, and then let me make a quick phone call. I've gotta make a phone call, it'll just take a minute. You wanna do me a favor and watch this suitcase for a minute? I know you don't have no clothes on, but the suitcase is locked so don't worry. Just for a minute while I make phone call. HEY! What the hell do you think you're doing? HEY!!!"

With a single yank and a twist, the cashier had ripped off the handle of the suitcase. Russell stared openmouthed at the ruined case. "What the hell did you do that for?"

The cashier fondled the red stone in her naval. "You can leave it here with me whiles you go and make yer phone call. Whadda ya think?"

I got a handle on this myself, thought Russell. *I don't need no suitcase handles to help me. I can carry it myself, without handles.* He could hardly believe it. It had all been so simple!

"That was damned smart of you," he sneered. "*I* shouldda thought of that. So you wanna make sure I don't go away, is that it? Well, lemmee tell you, you don't know what's in that suitcase. That's why I was carryin' it around all the time. And that's why I said, you bein' naked an' all, why I didn't wanna check it. My wife's in that suitcase. Yep! Doesn't look big enough, does it? Well, she's in there all right, all wrapped up like a case of Harold's underwear samples. Y'see, my wife's sister's husband Harold is married to my wife's sister Edith. It wasn't easy to get her in there!"

"I'll bet it wasn't," agreed the cashier. "So you want me to watch *her* and not the suitcase—is that it?" the cashier chuckled, handing him a tit. "And yet you trust me to open a pack of cigarettes for you when it's against the law. What kind of criminal do you think I am? Of course I'll watch her for you!"

"Gee, thanks!" Russell gave her tit a quick kiss and then on second thought, gave her other tit a kiss as well. "I'll be right back. You see, this phone call to Pittsburgh, it's right down the street. You ever been there? I hadn't realized how heavy it was until I put it down. Lots of years in there. Thanks a million! I just have to call my wife and tell her not to wait for me. My shoulder actually aches from carrying the damn thing around. Without my wife I really feel weightless and sort of free all over."

Russell tried to look into her eyes instead of her headlights. "You ever felt weightless before? It's the funniest damn feeling, like you're hungry and you're really not, or like you're lonely. Terribly lonely. What did you say? I wasn't listening."

"I asked you if you liked tomatoes," repeated the cashier. "Tomato pie."

"Oh... well..." Russell considered, rubbing his chin. Where was his mouth? His poor aching twitching mouth? It was here a minute ago. "If it was a la mode with soft vanilla ice cream, or if it's lilac color, I suppose it would be quite good and not so bad, eh? Heh-heh!"

"I know of a place down the street," said the cashier. "It's two blocks down."

"Sure," said Russell. "We can just leave the suitcase here, can't we? I mean, if it has no handles no one can take it. And the ticket man isn't even here anymore. Poor fella. He's probably too weak to lift a fly, let alone a body in a suitcase without a handle. And you know something?"

Russell moved closer, smelling her powder, smelling the soft mintiness of her breath. He could feel it on his face, could feel it the way it came and went every time she breathed in and breathed out. He could almost taste it. Why was he crying? Why were two big tears rolling down his cheeks, followed by two more?

What a baby he was! What a big crybaby! "You want to know something?" he whispered hoarsely. "I really was scared before. Honest! I was scared to death—scared of you, if you can believe it. But now I don't feel scared at all. In fact, now that you're naked, now that I know what's underneath that pretty blouse of yours and you gave me your suitcase to hold..."

It was soft and smooth and very light. Much lighter than he thought. Light as spun sugar. "Now that you're here," he sobbed, "like I said, I feel really great, and terribly free."

THEREFORE I AM

"Ms. Lorca, are you still there? Ms. Lorca? We seem to have a bad connection. As I was saying, congratulations! Ms. Lorca?"

"Yes, thank you, Mr. Proffit, I mean Moffit, I mean no, I mean yes, I'm—I'm still—of course I'm delighted. I'm stunned, in fact completely overwhelmed! Mr. Moffit, are you sure it's me, I mean that the winner is—"

Ms. Lorca, please don't underestimate your ability. You are a first class poet. A classy first-class poet, based on ahem your photo. Is that a recent one? There were 10, 872.6 submissions and we had to hire 54.75 additional judges and 10.5% came down with the swine flu just before—"

"Well actually, what I meant was, Mr. Moffitt, are you sure there aren't two Gracie Lorca's who might have submitted manuscripts titled—"

"*Eschatological Flakes*? Ms. Lorca, please! Be real. You will be receiving the proofs in the mail and the written contract for publication including percentages, royalties and all the rest of that s—, er, the legalities that attorneys ask for. If you would be good enough to return this document signed within ten days so that we can... and oh yes, we shall be using recycled paper of .600, quality number 'R' 1786. The binding will be Sebastian and Munchendorph, with a Wainscotting number of..."

Not that I *wouldn't* have wanted to win the Pen Quivers International Poetry Competition, but I already knew before I answered the phone that it was totally impossible. I'd never won anything except deodorant and hair spray in a supermarket raffle.

"...four thousand nine-hundred and forty-two point six," Mr. Moffitt continued. "Ms. Lorca, congratulations again! Good-byyyeee!"

Amazing, I thought. There are two Gracie Lorca's in the world and both are poets. Both submitted manuscripts to Pen Quivers International Poetry Contest with the exact same title... of course, the other Gracie Lorca might be a pen name. Mine was not. Or at least, it was me, or Me Nee, before I was married. When I married Walter Stevens, I'd become Gracie Stevens, but only for bank accounts, taxes, insurance, etc.

I wondered where she lived and what would happen when the Quivers discovered their error.

"Will the real Gracie Lorca please stand up?" I *was* already standing up, or at least one of them was, and the tea kettle was whistling.

I studied the lineup of tea bags, finally choosing OneUpper, since I was tired of WrungDry and was out of HeartFelt and LazyBone.

On the side of the OneUpper box, I read the ingredients: a blend of hibiscus root, dandelion fuzz, desiccated kelp, mistletoe berries and closet lint.

A quick check of my hard drive proved what I already knew: 1) the manuscript, *Eschatological Flakes*, did in fact exist, 2) it carried the byline of Gracie Lorca, and 3) if I was/were, in fact "that other" Gracie Lorca but had been contacted as the winner of the Pen Quivers International Poetry Contest, I did, in fact, exist. Or at least one of us did.

The only reason I'd decided to enter the contest was because I was tired of trying to prove I wasn't a loser. Why not try the opposite for a change, I'd decided. Why not make an out and out *effort* to *be* a loser and enjoy the experience of being right?

Number 1 Losers Point - No one who is anyone in this country reads poetry. Therefore, anyone who publishes it already knows it's a losing business. Loss of investment, loss of profit... Therefore, I knew had everything to lose by submitting a poetry manuscript to an international contest that would be flooded with entries from gifted and not so gifted poets struggling like me, to get their name in print.

Number 2 Losers Point - I knew the game. With a $5.00 submission fee and hundreds, possibly thousands of entries, it would be easy to cover the costs for publishing the winning manuscript, which was the prize. Also, Pen Quivers *had* to have a winner or the Better Business Bureau and Attorney General would call it Ponzi and take them to court.

What a great scheme. Five dollars multiplied by 10,872.6 manuscripts or maybe more... Why hadn't *I* thought of it?

Shoot the dice and pick a number. Any number. Up comes *Eschatological Flakes.*

I stared glumly at the snowballs of wadded nothings frothing out of the wastebasket. The icy block of paper next to my printer was as white as... as... blank. "Blank" as in *blank.*

How the idea first evolved is of no consequence. Maybe it began as a metaphor or a simile, or a simple aspiration: one sucked-in breath that exhaled to another until a sound evolved, evoking the word and the word, the meaning... and so, in the beginning...

Why not? I argued. Isn't it time to learn the truth, once and for all? "Game" and "gamble." The two words were interchangeable. And wasn't the abbreviation for "Number" "No."? *No,* meaning *nothing?* Nothing to lose, nothing to gain?

All this derivation effluvia was hardly original. I recall there were even several non-existent students who had made it all the way through four years of college via computerized matriculation, often graduating with honors and special citations before they were undiscovered.

How many blank canvases does one encounter in the world's highly prestigious art galleries and museums? Have I not marveled at the ingenuity of the wool-pulling charlatans who collect handsome fees for their splotches of paint, or simply for their "White on White"?

I would number the pages and place them in order, add a [blank] Table of Contents and include Acknowledgments of previously published [blank] poems. The [blank] collection would have a title—required for the Pen Quivers' files, so they could give it a number.

It took only a matter of days, minutes actually, before I finished the manuscript and sent it off.

I tried to picture my husband Walter's incredulity when I broke the news about winning, but could not. "So at last, after all that postage it paid off, and we can buy a McDonald's Whopper wrapper," he would gloat, unbelieving.

Then, the glee of Rafie and Tib, my six and eight year olds. "Gee Mom, you're famous! D'ya think you'll be on the *Today Show*? D'ya think they'll make a movie on you?"

No, it absolutely *could not* be a case of mistaken identity. Even if I had won *anything*, ever, I reminded myself, *even a Thanksgiving turkey in a church raffle,* my family would be proud of me. Every achievement of mine would be theirs, so how could I disappoint them? I could not let them down.

There was only one thing to do, I told myself firmly. I must sit down right now and write a book titled *Eschatological Flakes.* Or at least one poem with that title, so it could be included in the winning manuscript and quotable for the media.

In a single gulp I drained the rest of my Upper.

"You think you can get away with it, don't you?" croaked the green speckled creature glaring up at me from the bottom of the mug. "The truth will surface or I'm no amphibian. So just put *that* in your cup and drink it!"

"Oh Froggie," I moaned, "why can't I be a princess so I can be the genuine Me, the Real Gracie Lorca, the Pen Quiver's choice, the authentic Eschatological Flake? Why must I always be mistaken for somebody else?"

"Because my dear Gracie, you have to be. It is your destiny to be mistaken. And truthfully, you don't even have the froggiest notion of what the Quivers intends to publish. So when the proofs arrive and you open the package, when you discover who you are or have become—how will anyone be able to *live* with you?"

Froggie was right, so I took a cold shower and studied my naked image in the full-length mirror. "You are not just a poet," informed the middle-aged female body coldly appraising me.

"You are also an intelligent, perceptive et cetera et cetera. You have never trusted contests before. And knowing the odds in the poetry business added to the odds in the contest racket, the winning manuscript is probably not only flaky but corny. Right?"

"Right," I repeated.

No answer.

I tried again. "Is it better to go down in history as the author of Something or the Author of Nothing? Is it not better to have an opportunity to be nominated for the Nobel Prize, or—" I reached into the medicine cabinet and withdrew the slim, hand-sewn, ivory-colored volume, and opened to the first poem. Adjusting my reading glasses, I cleared my throat and rested my hands on the lectern.

"Blank as the blankest of all blanks," I began. It was nice giving a poetry reading in the bathroom. With all the tile and glass, the acoustics were remarkable.

It was, after all, the Quivers' mistake, not mine. And for all I know—what *do* I know about myself? I pondered, examining the progress of a corn removal on my left little toe. For all I knew, maybe I *had* written a collection of poetry titled... whoever said, or believed a poet lived in the world of reality? Weren't they supposed to be a little uh er...um... Think of Byron and Keats. Think of Dylan Thomas, Ezra Pound and Garcia Lorca. Hmmm.

Damn. No more corn pads in the medicine cabinet and I'd forgotten to pick up another pack at the pharmacy.

Straightening, I hobbled to the bedroom closet, snatched up my bathrobe and angrily flung it on. All this foolish deception had to stop. *I* knew who I was, even if no one else did.

The truth was the truth. I had never been known for creating anything extraordinary except barbecued chicken and chocolate brownies.

I had no choice. I was moral—or if I wasn't, at least my feet were on the ground, corn or no. So I would have to stand on them. I had no choice. They, or I, would have to turn themselves in.

Gracie looked up from the computer and pulled out a wad of Kleenex, blowing her nose and wiping her eyes. She hadn't realized until now that she was crying. Was she really so upset with the protagonist of her little story, so thoroughly immersed in the little drama she had created—the story of a mistaken identity that in this case verged on the tragic—merely because it involved the accidental winning of an international poetry contest?

Someone was ringing the doorbell.

The uniformed UPS man handed her a large flat package and signature pad. Gracie's heart skipped a beat when she moved the stylus across the screen. Nothing. No name at all.

"Sorry, Maam. Sometimes it don't work. Try it again."

She bore down harder, and there she was on the monitor: *Gracie Lorca.*

The package was from M.M. Moffit of the Quivers Poetry Society. She tore off the letter from the outside pocket and ripped it open.

Dear Ms. Lorca,

Enclosed are the proofs for your book, which we would like to have you...

Gracie sat down. She stood up. She sat down. How...? It was ludicrous! Absurd! Outrageous! Here before her, in the package she was now bringing into the kitchen to cut open with the kitchen shears, was the winning manuscript, *her* manuscript! It was ready to go to press bearing Her Name on the title page—Gracie—Gracie—Gracieeeeeeee, whistled the tea kettle.

Obviously the situation is out of hand, croaked Froggie.

"Yes indeed," she snapped, reaching for a OneUpper tea bag. Obviously. Obviously there is nothing to do but open the package and...

Gracie hacked at the string with a knife and tore off the wrapper, leafing through the first blank page to the second blank page to the third blank page to the fourth and fifth... Leaving a trail of blank sheets flying after her, she carried the rest of the manuscript to her desk and laid it next to the block of blank paper beside her printer.

She stared at it for a moment as if to verify its presence and the likenesses of the two stacks of blank paper. Then she let out a yell.

"You won, Gracie Lorca! You won!"

POSSIBLE PLOTS

I first noticed Bella shortly after we'd moved to another area of the city and I started to shop at a Safeway where she was a cashier. A pale scrawny-looking thing with a crooked nose and straight blonde hair, she seemed too quick and smart for her job.

It was something about the way her eyes and hands worked together, scanning, checking and bagging while her mind registered every detail of the customers moving through the line. One had the feeling that she was silently conversing with each of them, chatting about personal matters that she'd have no way of actually knowing about, unless these people were acquaintances, relatives or friends. They were not.

These customers were strangers. She didn't even know their names, and the only way they could have known hers was if they happened to notice it printed on the plastic card she wore above the left pocket of her blouse. "Bella."

I'm sure many of these shoppers would have used the self-serve kiosks instead of waiting in a cashier's line, but whenever Bella was at one of the registers they seemed to gravitate toward her lane. So did I, even when Bella's line was long and I could have checked out my items faster and been on my way much sooner.

I never noticed whether Bella was married, although these days rings on a woman's fingers meant nothing. Also, because she was so thin and underdeveloped I assumed she might have been only a few years older than my teenage daughter. Maybe she was a college student, or saving for a future education. Clearly, Bella didn't belong here in the supermarket.

It was a surprise one day to notice as she was checking out my groceries, a definitive hump beneath her cashier's smock. My eyes were automatically drawn to Bella's left hand. There they were on her fourth finger. Two wire-thin bands, one bearing a tiny white stone. No embellishments, merely two rings and the stone.

As the weeks grew and somehow I felt compelled to seek out Bella's cashier lane even when I came to the store for only a couple items, the hump became more noticeable. For some reason, I felt extreme pleasure in confirming to myself the fact that she was obviously pregnant.

Why should I be anything more than idly curious, I wondered. What was it about this girl that was so fascinating, and why did she seem so out of place here in the supermarket?

Never missing a beat, Bella proceeded to efficiently check out my grocery items, never ceasing to carry on her internal conversations with me and other customers as we passed through the line.

What was she saying? Why did it seem important? How COULD it be important, if I didn't know what the conversation was about? Was this merely my imagination?

Soon I found myself rummaging through kitchen cupboards looking for items I might not need now but would be running out of soon... well within the next six months maybe, I admitted to myself. Any excuse I could find that would take me to the supermarket and to Bella's checkout line—I had already noted her work schedule. Any excuse that would give me another opportunity to see Bella and experience her silent conversations.

Apparently I wasn't the only customer who had sensed something unusual about the girl. One day when I decided I could use another tube of toothpaste, I'd just stationed myself behind a woman who was already checking out her groceries in Bella's line. The woman looked up from the shopping cart she was emptying and asked: "So when is it due?"

Bella glanced at the woman. "In two months."

"Oh my," declared the woman, raising her voice. Her expensive perfume wafted toward me, and I picked up "wealthy" from the woman's general appearance. Impeccable French twist coiffure, manicure and makeup; stylish coral-colored velour jumpsuit and strappy 6-inch coral-colored heels. "You're much too small if your baby's almost due. And too thin."

I felt the blood rush to my head. *What business did this woman have, butting in on this girl's affairs?*

The woman continued, "You need to start taking some nutrients, now, if you want to save that baby."

She leaned forward, placing one of her coral-colored nails on Bella's arm. "I'm telling you, honey, you've got to do something now, before it's too late!" The woman's voice rose to a shrill pitch.

Anger curdled in my stomach and rose to my throat. Before I could stop myself, I retorted hotly, "What makes *you* such an expert about someone else's baby?"

The woman turned to me, her face flushed, a strand of dyed blonde hair flying loose from her lacquered up-do. "I should know," she snapped. "I of all people should know what's going to happen if this girl doesn't do something NOW."

Several customers turned their heads in our direction and one of the checkout supervisors strolled over.

Bella nodded and smiled at the supervisor, indicating that everything was under control. "Yes, I'm sure you *should* be concerned about such things," she said evenly to the woman. "Thank you."

The woman's jaw dropped open and she turned visibly red. Her shame and embarrassment were evident.

"It's all right," Bella reassured me, glancing in my direction. She turned back to the woman and finished packing her groceries.

"Have a good day," she said to the woman, handing her the receipt. Without another word, she pulled her plastic bags from the shopping cart and clacked out of the store.

Still seething, I emptied my cart of items onto the conveyor belt. "What was that all about?" I asked.

"You are very kind," Bella said.

Our eyes met and I felt a powerful energy pass between us.

Bella went on maternity leave shortly afterward so I started frequenting another Safeway that was more conveniently located.

Then one day two or three months later, I was on my way home from a meeting and in the area of "Bella's Safeway." I was completely out of rice milk, one of my staples and I knew this market carried the brand I used.

To my surprise and delight, Bella was back at work. She looked the same as before she'd started to grow the pouch in front, but I sensed something different about her.

"Well!" I exclaimed before I could stop myself, "how is the new little one? Is it a boy or a girl?"

Her hand paused on the rice milk carton and she straightened. "It was a boy," she said in a small thin voice. "But he died. He didn't live."

The lights went out. The stage darkened except for the illuminated box of milk in her hand, an illustration on the back depicting a happy family seated around a breakfast table, the baby boy in the high chair gurgling merrily and waving his arms as he reached for the bowl his mother was about to place before him.

"I'm sorry," I murmured.

"It's all right," she said, gazing at me directly as she methodically continued bagging my rice milk.

As I returned her gaze, I really knew it was all right, that she was telling the truth. It was I who was feeling sad, feeling sorry for her. For some reason, I had been itching to "fix" her life, to "help" her. But she needed no help. She needed nothing because she already had everything she wanted and needed.

If tragedy or misfortunate should strike, unlike most people, Bella had it covered. She was a great teacher.

Once a doctor friend, a pediatrician, shared with me a story about what had happened that day at the hospital. He'd been called into emergency to examine a newborn who had just been washed and cleaned.

A teenager had become pregnant and somehow she'd been able to conceal her pregnancy from her family. No one knew the details, but I suppose it's possible to hide a bulge if a person is large anyway, and wears smocks and baggy clothes. Also, she lived in an area of the city where parents, if there were two of them, were seldom home. Probably the girl was gone from home most of the time herself.

When it was time for the baby to be born, the girl had entered the outhouse—in this neighborhood indoor plumbing was rare—and proceeded to give birth to the baby. Somehow she'd managed to sever the umbilical cord and then, having no use for the baby, tossed it into the hole.

It was discovered later that day by the girl's mother when she heard a faint cry emerging from the outhouse.

The baby not only survived but my pediatrician friend said it was rated a number 10, meaning it was in all ways perfect.

My husband and I became good friends with Iola and Evan Reed. Iola was a concert artist, a soprano, and Evan was head of a large software company. They had everything going for them: successful careers, an exciting life, and love. They were a stunning couple and one could immediately sense the fire between the two of them.

Iola desperately wanted to have a child but after visiting several fertility specialists they learned it was a chemical problem with Evan. To date medical science had not come up with a solution.

How could life be so unfair? I found myself asking. One could picture a whole family of little Iola's and Evans growing up at their California estate with the best education, the best opportunities.... and surely their children would be gifted like their parents.

With her usual grace and skill, Iola would have easily embraced motherhood and continued with her career. Likewise, Evan would have modified his lifestyle if necessary, to be a father who was truly present for his children.

Iola's New York debut was sensational. Soon she was singing with major orchestras and chamber ensembles. Every couple of months or so we used to go out to dinner and theater together, but then Iola booked an international tour and was away from California for six months. We were also traveling a great deal at that time, so we lost touch with each other.

One day Iola called to inform me that she was pregnant and the baby was due in five and a half months. She said she hadn't told anyone until now because it had been a shaky beginning and the doctor had ordered her to rest and cut back on her activities. Now, however, there seemed to be no problem. The baby was growing and she was feeling wonderful.

Possibly because Iola was such a knockout—a real "babe"—and her career was at its peak, rumors started flying. The media was always looking for celebrity scoops and Iola's career inevitably brought her together with many other hi-octane artists. "If you don't have fire yourself, what can you deliver to your audience?" Iola was fond of joking.

One of Iola and Evan's friends was an acclaimed choreographer, Jean Robert from France, who used to stay in their guest house when he was performing in the California area. Evan's business took him out of town a great deal and when he was gone, often Iola and Jean would go places together. They had been photographed at chic Beverly Hills cafés or strolling down Rodeo Drive, attending opera and symphony galas together... For the past six months, Evan had been traveling and was rarely home. Jean was working on a film and he had accepted the Reeds' invitation to stay at their estate during that time.

I heard the stories but didn't listen. I had the highest regard for Iola and had no desire to participate in any rumor mills. Yet I couldn't deny the timing was right. Evan was away, Jean was staying in their guest house... I also knew enough about Evan's medical problem. It was highly unlikely that he could impregnate any female.

If Iola and Evan had heard the rumors, and no doubt they had, they had chosen to ignore them. They seemed more devoted to each other than ever, and now with their forthcoming event, excitedly they chattered about it with us whenever we got together. It was going to be a perfect baby! Iola had cancelled all of her engagements for the coming year and was taking meticulous care of herself... watching her diet, resting, exercising... With the discipline of a performing artist, she followed to a letter all the instructions of the doctor and other birthing experts.

Nine full months, six days and only a few hours later, my phone rang. It was Iola, informing me that her baby had just been born with the umbilical cord wound around its neck. Strangled.

"There was no way of rescuing it in time," she said dully.

Shortly after, Evan and Iola filed for divorce and Iola moved to San Francisco where she took a job working in a florist's shop. She never sang again.

The *New York Times* had a story recently about Evan's remarriage to the daughter of a wealthy oil tycoon.

Carol Adler, MFA's first ghost-written book listing her name as co-editor, *Why Am I Still Addicted? A Holistic Approach to Recovery*, was endorsed by Deepak Chopra, M.D., and published by McGraw-Hill. Other publications include three novels, four books of poetry, and well over 200 poems in literary journals. She has ghostwritten over 40 non-fiction and fiction works for a number of professionals in the education, health care and human potential industries.

Carol is President of Dandelion Books, LLC, www.dandelion-books.com
of Mesa, Arizona; a full service publishing company. She is also President and CEO of Dandelion Enterprises, Inc., www.write-to-publish-for-profit.com.

Her business experience includes co-ownership of a Palm Beach, FL public relations company and executive management positions in two U.S. rejuvenation and mind/body wellness corporations, for which she founded publishing divisions.

Carol has served as editor of several poetry and literary magazines. Her career experience includes extensive teaching of college-level creative and business writing, and conducting of writing work-shops in prisons, libraries, elementary, junior and high schools, and senior citizen centers.

She is also a Certified Hypnotherapist and Source Integration Therapist and for 12 years was an officer of the Arizona Society for Professional Hypnosis.

Recent Adler titles are: *Writers, Authors & Dreamweavers: I Heard Your Call For Help - How to Write Non-Fiction, Fiction, Poetry, Memoirs, Children's Stories...and More; Do You Really Need To Write A Book?; Shaelot: Questions* [poetry]; *Arioso, Selected Poems* [poetry]; *Slouching Past Bethlehem* [novel]; *The Extinctive Life* [novel]; and *Naked In Daylight* [poetry].

Soon forthcoming are two collections of poetry, *Jesus & The Tooth Fairy/Free Radicals*, and *You, Woman!* She is also working on a new novel, *Inquiring Minds,* and a book about Source Integration Therapy.

Carol Adler's Websites:

www.write-to-publish-for-profit.com
www.ghostwritercaroladler.com
www.lettersofcreation.com
www.dandelion-books.com

www.ingramcontent.com/pod-product-compliance
Lightning Source LLC
Chambersburg PA
CBHW080740250626

47170CB00010B/2893